A FACE WITHOUT
A REFLECTION

A FACE WITHOUT A REFLECTION

Linda Lee Bowen

ISBN: 0692999493
ISBN 13: 9780692999493
Library of Congress Control Number: 2017919099
CreateSpace Independent Publishing Platform
North Charleston, South Carolina
All scriptural quotations are taken from the Holy Bible, New International Version®, NIV®. Copyright ©1973, 1978, 1984, 2011 by Biblica, Inc.® Used by permission. All rights reserved worldwide.

To my sons,
Casey and Tyler,
and my sister, Sharon.
I love you more
than the whole, wide world.

And to Neal.
Thank you for everything
that was very, very good.
It's all that matters.

For now we see only a reflection as in a mirror; then we shall see face to face. Now I know in part; then I shall know fully, even as I am fully known. And now these three remain: *faith, hope and love*. But the greatest of these is love.

—1 Corinthians 13:12–13 (NIV)

CONTENTS

PART I
GRACE FALLS

CHAPTER

One	Ending Eleven	3
Two	That Which Is Perfection	11
Three	The Gift	19
Four	As Spirit Sleeps	40
Five	No Way to End A Day	52
Six	Faith, Hope, And Love You Stew	67
Seven	The Day Things Went Horribly Wrong	84
Eight	Off with Her Head	107
Nine	A Disappointment to Everyone	116
Ten	The Problem with Otterhounds	125
Eleven	The Twelfth Day of June	137
Twelve	From Tomb to Womb	148

PART II
U-R-HERE

CHAPTER

Thirteen	Born Again	153
Fourteen	U-R-Here, But Who Are You?	157
Fifteen	Meeting Daddy	163
Sixteen	Meeting Micah	166
Seventeen	Whatever Is Right, Whatever Is Pure	175
Eighteen	The Finder of Seekers	182
Nineteen	Gone Fishin'	188
Twenty	And Then There Were Four	201
Twenty-One	Farewell, Old Friend	212
Twenty-Two	The Enemy Is Fear	218
Twenty-Three	The Way	224
Twenty-Four	The Truth	233
Twenty-Five	The Life	240
Epilogue		245
About the Author		249

PART I
GRACE FALLS

CHAPTER 1

ENDING ELEVEN

I was at the end of my eleventh year on earth and turning twelve was only hours away—well...turning twelve in the natural, anyway. But I'll tell you about that later. Let's just say that on the night before my twelfth birthday, I had no way of knowing that in a few short weeks, my entire world would come crashing down and everything I ever believed, trusted, or loved would be permanently and irrevocably changed. If I'd had an inkling as to what lay ahead, I would have clung to every word, every gesture, and every movement my mother made that night as she sat in the faded-blue armchair next to my bed and began a tale she would never end.

"Did you know," she asked as she tucked me in, "that there once was a girl who had no reflection?"

"She had no reflection? That's weird! Was she invisible?"

"No," she replied matter-of-factly. "She wasn't invisible." Her bright eyes twinkled as she stood to turn down the light.

"Was she blind?" I asked, trying to figure out where the story was going.

"Oh no!" she answered, apparently distracted by the pile of clothes I'd left scattered on the floor. "She was blessed with twenty-twenty vision and saw others and everything around her with incredible clarity. Far better than most!"

"Hmmm." I rolled onto my back to stare at the shadows on the ceiling. I wanted to appear as though I was giving the story careful consideration, but the truth was, I was trying to ignore the sight of my mother picking up my things. I checked on her progress from the corner of my eye. When it looked as though the room was in order, I decided it was safe to look at her again.

"Does that mean that everyone saw everyone else, but no one saw themselves?" I asked, without acknowledging her efforts.

She sat sideways in her favorite blue chair and rested her tiny bare feet on one of the arms. My mother was a petite woman, who was perfectly proportioned and in excellent shape, although she paid very little attention to the way she looked and didn't care if anyone else did. But it was impossible for people not to notice her. She was a natural beauty who never wore makeup or styled her shoulder-length dirty-blond hair—unless you would call a ponytail a "style." Her wardrobe reflected her plain, no-nonsense approach and consisted mostly of T-shirts, sweats, and jeans. And when she absolutely had to wear shoes, her preference was work boots or flip-flops. But it was a warm night in May. So, her feet were naked.

"Well…" she began as she considered my question, "no. Everyone else saw their own reflections as well as the reflections of others. Just like you or me. But we must remember that mirrors can be deceiving. And what everyone thought they saw when they gazed into their mirrors often wasn't there at all."

"Huh?" I propped myself up on both elbows and scowled. "I don't get it. Mirrors don't lie."

My mother's hands were clasped tight to her chest. "Ah!" she replied, pointing one finger into the air. "But the truth is that much of what we see every day includes a measure of what we assume something should look like. So, we don't often see the whole picture. Only what's on the surface. We miss a lot of beauty that way."

I flopped down hard on the bed and threw the covers over my head. The last thing I wanted to hear was a lecture on how "beauty comes from within" and "it's not how we look that's important but how we feel." I had been feeling pretty lousy of late, and I put all the blame on the way I looked. I hated mirrors and everything about them. All they ever showed me was a fat, round-faced girl whose hands and feet were growing faster than the rest of her body. I felt like a freak. Hair had appeared in places I'd never even paid attention to, and if that was not enough, my chest was getting all puffy…like I was starting to grow breasts. Breasts! Who needs breasts? Who even wants them? I didn't know what was happening to me, but I didn't like it one bit. Of course, I was too embarrassed to talk to my mom about it. For one thing, I was afraid she might flip out or take me to the doctor or, even worse, tell me it was just my imagination and I was "beautiful inside and out." As if that ever helped anything!

"Argh!" I grumbled from inside my tent.

"It's complicated," my mother said, peeking under the sheets.

I didn't look at her, but I knew she was making goofy faces. That was what she did whenever I was angry about something. She made goofy faces or pretended she didn't hear me. Sometimes she'd leave the room for a while and then come back in and talk about something that was completely off the subject. I hated that. It was as if she thought I was too stupid to remember what I was mad about or that it wasn't important enough to discuss.

I shut my eyes as tightly as I could and snarled at the sheets until she retreated. It was quiet for a moment. Had she left? Then she plopped her feet on top of the covers, and they landed so hard that they made the bed squeak. Who plants their feet on a bed like that? No one. That's who! Unless they were trying to make it very obvious that they were still there, which totally annoyed me, especially since it was getting stuffy in my hiding place and I needed a breath of fresh air. But now I didn't want to give her the satisfaction of coming out. Even though I'd forgotten what I was mad about. And *that* made me feel stupid.

"Well"—she sighed loudly—"I guess if you don't want to hear what I have to say about mirrors, there's no sense in going on with my story."

Oh…my…word! She was pouting. I hated it when she pouted. It was so childish. Pouting meant I'd hurt her feelings, and hurting her feelings was the worst thing I could do. It made me feel like an awful person and a terrible daughter. I wanted to tell her that, but instead I sucked it up, took a deep breath, and slowly pulled back the sheets.

"I'm sorry, Mommy," I whispered, with my mouth still under the covers. "I want to hear your story."

I caught a glimpse of her sad eyes and drooping mouth, and it was more than I could handle. So I mustered up the extra-big, wide-eyed grin that I knew she was waiting for before fully emerging from my inner sanctum.

"Please, Mommy! Please!" I pleaded. "I really, really want to hear it." As usual, this did the trick, and we both smiled as she pulled her feet back onto the chair and found her comfy place.

"Okay!" she said, fully reenergized. "Let's see...where was I? Oh yes. Mirrors!"

If there was one thing my mother was good at, it was bouncing back. Of course, she'd had a lot of practice.

"The thing is...mirrors can be deceptive. But not for the girl without a reflection! Not knowing what she looked like gave her a wonderful advantage over everyone else, for she saw the world around her for what it was, and she instinctively knew her place in it. She was completely unencumbered by a preconceived notion as to how something *should* look and was quite content with how it *did* look."

"What does 'uncucumbered' mean?" I knew that wasn't the word, of course. But I felt like making my mother laugh. And she did!

"'Unencumbered' means to be free of obstruction. In this case it means that although she was unable to see reflections, there was nothing that blocked her vision of anyone or anything around her. In fact, her vision was so keen, it was as though all her senses were wrapped up in her sight."

"Wow!" I rolled on my back and tucked my hands under my head. "It sounds kind of cool to be able to taste and smell something just by looking at it."

I took a few exaggerated whiffs of the air and licked my lips, trying to imagine what that would be like.

"Argh!" I growled as I shot up like a rocket. "What if I was all dorky and goofy looking, and I never knew it?" I pulled my legs underneath me and sat on the heels of my feet as I leaned toward my startled mother for answers. "What if my eyes were crossed or I had a really huge nose? What if I had buck teeth and a million freckles?" My fingers danced across my face, planting freckles like falling drops of rain. "People would make fun of me all the time, and I wouldn't even know why."

"Hmm," she muttered with a smirk. "That's an interesting thought. We should keep it in mind."

It seemed to me that if she'd been paying attention, she would have heard the air rushing out of the balloon she just poked a giant hole in by dismissing my valid contribution. This was, after all, the moment in my mother's stories that I lived for: the all-too-rare opportunity to add logic and reason to her wildly creative fairy tales that might, in some small way, validate my existence by proving that my ideas were as valuable as hers. Even if they weren't as entertaining. I didn't want her to know I felt deflated, so I pushed back the blankets with the heels of my feet and rearranged the pillows to make more space for moving around. Lying down was out of the question.

"Now, in the case of Mira," she began, "not knowing what she looked like when she was very young didn't matter to her at all. For one thing, she had no way of knowing she was not like everyone else. She assumed if she couldn't see herself, no one else saw themselves either. This was a reasonable assumption, of course, as it is not the kind of thing that comes up in the everyday conversation of a small child. So, Mira was completely unaware that she was, quite possibly, the only sighted person who had ever lived who didn't know what she looked like. It wasn't that this phenomenon was a secret; it simply was not important enough to mention."

"Wait a minute!" I halted her with outstretched arms. "Her name was Mirror?" It didn't seem like a terribly clever name, and I was quick to call her on it.

"No." She laughed. "Not Mirror. *Mira*. *M-i-r-a*. It's a shortened version of her real name, Krasimira. It's Slovakian, and it means 'beautiful peace.'"

"Beautiful peace. I like that."

My mother's eyes were smiling. "I thought you would," she said.

"But how could she...how could Krasimira...have beautiful peace if she didn't even know what she looked like?"

I sat in limbo, waiting for my mother's response. I was not at all like her. I could never be comfortable in a world that didn't make perfect sense. To me, things were either black or white, and there was no room for gray areas. If she were to successfully stretch my logical brain far enough to grasp the unimaginable, she must do it ever so slowly, gently casting her extravagant ideas out as far as she could, yet never beyond my grasp.

"Well," she began, as she lifted the covers for me to slide underneath, "I suppose I could try to answer your questions all night long." She fluffed the pillows to make them irresistible for my tired head. "Or I could start the story and see where it leads us. What would be your pleasure, Miss Johnson?"

I pulled the blankets under my chin and held on to them tightly as she leaned over and tucked me in.

"The story," I conceded happily.

"Well, all righty then! The story it is."

CHAPTER 2

THAT WHICH IS PERFECTION

A gentle breeze swept across the room from the open window and sent the sheer, diaphanous curtains dancing in the air. Mother settled into her old blue chair and placed an imaginary book in her lap. She held the pages of obligatory content under the thumb of her left hand as she fixed her gaze on the invisible text before her.

"Chapter one." She lifted her eyes for a moment to ensure she had my attention. I smiled as she read the words that were printed in her head.

"Neither long ago nor far away, there was a beautiful young girl named Krasimira, who lived with her mother, father, and maternal grandmother in the only house on the only hill in a tiny village known as U-R-Here. They were a remarkable family who, long before Krasimira was even born, had earned the reputation of being the happiest people who ever lived, as they were always smiling and never seemed to want or need anything more than precisely what they had."

"Were they very, very rich?" I asked from beneath the covers.

Mother continued as though I'd not interrupted her.

"It's not that they were rich. Heavens, no! But it's not that they were poor. Not at all! They were simply con- tent. And that was something everyone from Anywhere and Everywhere wanted to be but didn't know how to be it. They thought they would be happy if they had bigger houses, shinier cars, or the latest and greatest gizmo or whizzbang they'd seen on commercials and in magazines. But this was never the case, as buying more than what they needed often ended badly, as people from Anywhere and Everywhere were never satisfied with what they had and always wanted more. To them, there was no such thing as 'enough.'

"'Those who rely on the One Who Provides have all they ever need,' Krasimira's father would say.

"And relying on the One Who Provides worked extreme- ly well for the perfect family, as they counted everything as a blessing and gave thanks for it all. It's what made them so very happy in their not-too-big-not-too-small house that suited their needs just fine. And because they were happy, they wanted other people to be happy too. So their door was always open to friends and strangers alike. And the people from Anywhere and Everywhere and even Beyond would leave their great big houses, jump in their shiny new cars, and travel up the winding road that led to the only house on the only hill in U-R-Here, just to be with Krasimira's family.

"Someone once said that people were drawn to the house because there was always something wonderful cooking on the stove and an extra place setting at the table. And that was certainly true! They dined on food that was delectably delicious and deliriously divine. Beef seared, roasted, braised, or stewed; perfectly poached poultry; fish grandly grilled; seafood battered, baked, stuffed, or sautéed. All the ingredients were as fresh as the morning and made by the loving hands of Mira's mother and Grammy, who were affectionately known by one and all as 'the Two.' But it wasn't the food that fed their bellies that brought folks back time and time again. It was the light of pure love that fed their hungry spirits and filled their empty souls until they were full and overflowing with immeasurable joy."

I twirled a strand of hair around my finger as I tried to imagine what it would be like if everyone was happy all the time; but I stopped when I thought of some very sour people forcing a smile. I was glad it wasn't my job to keep them happy.

"Naturally, no one ever wanted to leave the house on the hill. For when it was time to return to their much bigger houses filled with a whole lot of stuff, they discovered that they were, in fact, quite empty. This made them unhappy as well as confused, as they didn't understand what the house on the hill had that theirs didn't. So, they went out and purchased more things they thought would fill their hearts with joy. But what they were looking for can't be bought at any price.

"'A house is nothing more than a house,' Krasimira's father would say. 'It's the love inside that makes it a home.'" My mother smiled and nodded her head in agreement.

"Krasimira's parents were rich with love for each other as well as for all humankind. It was a gift, of course, and one for which they were truly grateful. They worked hard, helped others, and poured love over everyone they met. The only thing that was missing from their lives was a child. On the day they learned they were to become parents, they were so overwhelmed by this long-awaited blessing that they prayed to the One Who Provides, thanking Him, for three days straight. They didn't eat. They didn't sleep. They just gave thanks. As they prepared for the impending birth of their miraculous child, it appeared that the whole earth was awaiting her arrival in joyful anticipation. With so much love around them, it should not be a surprise that Krasimira was born on the most beautiful day that ever was. There wasn't a single cloud in the azure sky as the sun shone down and warmed the lush green earth. The world was in full bloom, and the air was still and fragrant with the scent of lilac, roses, and new life. It was the perfect day to bear the perfect child."

"But she wasn't perfect!" I protested as I bolted straight up in bed once again. "Remember? She couldn't see herself, so she wasn't perfect."

"Stay with me, darling. There's no need to jump the gun."

I sighed, dropped back on my pillow, and pulled the blanket under my chin.

"Krasimira was perfect in every way that mattered," Mother said with a wise grin. "She was born with eyes that were emerald green and lips that had a lovely pink blush. When she cried her first breath of life, it sounded as if the angels were singing. She had been given ten fingers, ten toes, and just the slightest hint of wispy auburn hair that would one day be her crowning glory. But what her beaming parents didn't know on that miraculous day was that this glorious babe would never see her own green eyes, or the way her lovely hair framed her delicate heart-shaped face. For Krasimira was born without a reflection. She had a perfectly good image, of course. She was simply unable to see it."

She gave me a wink, but I ignored her signal and was up on one elbow, ready to strike.

"Whoa! Her own parents didn't know she couldn't see herself?"

"Of course not, dear. She was just a baby. All they saw was how precious she was."

She looked down at her lap as though she were about to read more from her imaginary book, but I was out from under the covers sitting cross-legged on the bed. I held up one hand, warning her to stop.

"Okay," I interrupted. "I get that. But what about later? Did they know about her reflection later?"

"I've got this, kiddo," she said with a wink.

I let out a sigh and then wiggled my feet under the sheets and plopped my head down on the pillows once again. The journey was in the hands of the one with the plan.

"Naturally the child's minor imperfection was imperceptible when she was an infant and not at all relevant as she began to grow. After all, Mira was a truly blissful child who was extraordinary in all the things that mattered. She was filled with joy, kindness, goodness, gentleness, faithfulness, patience, and love. Her father adored the very ground she stepped upon and devoted himself to assuring she was safe and secure in the place that was called U-R-Here. Her mother doted on her from the moment she was born, making certain she was well bathed, well fed, and well cared for, as all mothers do. And Grammy, who wanted her precious Mira to be wise, happy, and at peace in all things, read stories to her from the Word, as it was the only book she would ever need.

"'The secret to a happy life is written in these pages,' Grammy would say. 'It teaches us how to give as well as receive love. We must read the Word and practice these lessons each and every day that we may be abundantly blessed.'

"And so it was that Mira's family practiced the art of giving to receive, and in doing so, they were consistently surprised and delighted by blessings from the One Who Provides. And they were never, ever disappointed.

"'Love is the key to happiness,' Mira's father once mused. 'But great treasures await those who are willing to give them away.'"

I raised myself up again and was about to ask her why we didn't have a book that gave the secrets to happiness, when my mother hushed me with a finger to her lips.

"Mira loved caring for the earth and all living things. She cared for her garden and every beautiful flower that grew there. She cared for the animals, birds, and bees, calling each one by name. She cared for the brook, the river, and the stream. She kept them free from anything that might harm those living in their waters. Caring was what made her happy, and her happiness made her beautiful. Little Mira saw goodness and beauty in all things great and small, and the beauty that she saw was reflected on her. This was something that anyone who ever met her could see, and people often said, 'Mira, you are the most beautiful child in all the earth.'

"Mira would reply, 'Why, thank you! You are full of beauty as well.'

"Her lovely heart was filled with joy, as she knew beauty was something one felt when they gazed upon things they loved. It cannot be seen in a mirror; it resides in your heart. And, of course, mirrors were quite useless to Mira, anyway. It didn't matter if she stood before a mirror or if someone else did. Mira could not see a reflection. Not hers. Not anyone else's. I suppose there are many people today who would not agree, but this was, in fact, a great treasure to possess. On the day that Mira's mother and Grammy realized that their most beloved child could not see a reflection, they decided to keep this truth a secret until she was completely secure with her inner beauty.

"'After all,' Mira's mother declared, 'nothing good has ever come from gazing at oneself in a mirror.' And she was right."

Mother made a gesture as if she were closing the book. This was her way of telling me the story was over for the night and it was time for sleep.

"Aww!" I moaned. "Just a little bit more?"

"I'm afraid not, my sleepy one. Tomorrow is a very big day."

"Oh yes! It's my birthday."

"It sure is. And it promises to be a picture-perfect day, just for you. This time tomorrow, you'll be twelve years old. But tonight, you're still only eleven, and you need to get some sleep." My mother smiled as she turned off the light, tucked the covers around me, and brushed the hair away from my face.

"Mommy," I said with my eyes already closed, "do you think Mira is perfect?"

"Yes, honey, I do." As I drifted off to sleep, I heard her say, "Just like you."

CHAPTER 3

THE GIFT

T he morning sun was shining through my window, and birds were singing in the trees. I opened my eyes to the morning light and announced to the world, "It's my birthday!" I jumped out of bed and followed the aroma of bacon frying in the kitchen.

The sound of my feet thumping against the wooden floors announced my arrival, and I jumped into my mother's open arms as she twirled me around and said, "Happy birthday, my wonderful daughter!"

She kissed me on my cheek. Tiny ripples of joy washed over me as I held her tightly around her neck.

"Thank you, Mommy."

"Thank you, Lily Johnson. If it weren't for you, I would have nothing to celebrate every tenth day of May."

I giggled at my mother's words, knowing what they were leading up to. I'd heard the story of the day I was born every year, and although I knew it by heart, I was happy to hear it again.

"You're quite welcome," I said, playing along.

I took my seat at the table while she poured me a glass of orange juice and continued my birthday story. She looked at the clock on the wall and then down to the watch on her wrist.

"This time, twelve years ago," she said, tapping the watch with her finger, "you weren't yet on this earth."

I took a sip of orange juice and then sat on both hands and waited for my story to be served. Mother took several strips of crisp bacon from the frying pan and placed them on a paper towel. Then she turned up the heat on the stove and poured perfect circles of batter onto the griddle.

"It was May 10," she said, without missing a beat, "the day I was due to give birth. But the very smart doctor told me just two days earlier that I was not nearly ready to have a baby, so he decided to take a long weekend away with his family and said he would see me the following week. Well, he clearly didn't know who he was dealing with because Lillian Landis Johnson knew that it was May 10 and that she was expected to make an appearance."

Mother turned from her cooking to give me a nod and a wink. "And you, Miss Johnson, are not one who disappoints."

I nodded my head and took a sip of orange juice. If there was one thing I knew about myself, it was that I never, ever disappointed anyone—which was not an easy thing to do. But I had learned this truth from my mother, of course, who had said these words to me thousands of times and always seemed pleased when I acknowledged them.

"So even though the very smart doctor thought you were going to wait until his long weekend was over, you decided to—"

"Stick to the original plan!" I chimed in on cue.

"That's right." My mother chuckled in mock surprise. "And so, at 1:23 a.m., I called the doctor to tell him you were ready to be born.

"He didn't believe me, of course, but he didn't want this very expectant mother to be anxious while he was away. He told me to come to his office, and when he had a closer look, he said, 'You're absolutely right, Miss Johnson.' Then he sent me straight to the hospital."

"That's when the really nice lady at the front desk saw you, right, Mom?"

"Oh yes! She was so sweet and so kind. I couldn't have hoped for a warmer welcome. She could tell right away that I was about to become a mother, so she quickly grabbed a wheelchair and took me up to the fifth floor, where she said, 'Good-bye, dear! Best of luck.'

"I waved good-bye as she stepped into the elevator, and a lovely young nurse checked me into a room as I waited for the doctor to arrive."

"What time was it then, Mommy?"

"It was 4:31 a.m., and I knew without a doubt that you were on your way. So I climbed into bed and started telling you how much I loved you and how excited I was to know I would see you soon."

"You didn't know if I was a boy or a girl, right?"

"I did not. And it didn't matter to me one little bit. I love surprises!"

"But you're glad that I'm a girl."

"Oh yes, I'm very glad you're a girl—a beautiful girl born on a perfect day in May."

She hummed as she poured maple syrup onto a stack of buttered blueberry pancakes and then placed a single candle in the middle and sang "Happy Birthday to You."

"It's time to make a big wish, Lily Johnson! You are twelve years old today, so you can wish for anything you want. Just remember to keep your eyes closed and try to imagine what your birthday wish would look like. When you have a crystal-clear image in your mind, you can open your eyes and blow out the candle. But," she warned, "don't open them too soon, or your wish won't have time to come true."

I was well acquainted with the rules for wish making, one of which was never to say your wish out loud. But the most important one was to keep your eyes closed. Breaking the rules could keep your wish from coming true, and this was one wish I wanted with all my heart.

I kept my eyes shut tight as I imagined the only thing I ever really wanted in my short life: a puppy. I saw him clearly. It was as if he were sitting right in front of me. He had brown-and-white fur that looked a little like shag carpet but was soft to touch. His long, floppy ears were almost comical and, like his paws, seemed too big for the rest of him. I had imagined him with dark, sad eyes that brightened up the moment he saw me. I could almost feel his tail wagging as he planted kisses that left the smell of puppy breath all over my face. I was afraid that when I opened my eyes, my wish would disappear forever. I couldn't bear such a grave disappointment. I kept them shut tight until the image began to fade, and I prepared myself for a less-than-miraculous gift. But when I opened my eyes...he was there.

"Oh, Mommy!" I squealed in disbelief. "My wish came true! It came true!"

Mother handed me the puppy she must have kept hidden in the barn, and we both laughed as he wiggled up my belly to lick my face. I laughed so hard that I cried and nearly fell off my chair. I didn't ever remember being so happy.

My mother was incredibly happy too. She laughed as the dog planted big, wet puppy kisses all over me. Then she clapped her hands in unbridled applause and shouted, "Hooray!" as if she simply could not contain herself any longer.

"You know what, Lily?" she asked as she knelt beside us. "I think you're his wish come true too."

I held him close to my heart and said, "I'll love him forever." And I meant it. "Where did he come from? How did you find him? Does he have a name? What kind of dog is he?" I abandoned my birthday breakfast and sat on the kitchen floor as my new puppy climbed clumsily on and off my lap.

"Well," she began, "a business associate of Mrs. Robbins has a farm not far from here. They have an otterhound who recently had a litter of four puppies: three females and one male. He's just twelve weeks old, and this is the first time he's been away from his mother. Her name is Molly. They aren't sure who the father is, but I suspect it might be a border collie that lives nearby. He was on the property when I went over to meet Molly and again when I picked up the puppy. Both he and Molly are very friendly, so the pup should have a good temperament. Molly's owner says he is very playful and that he loves chasing rabbits, although he never gets close enough to catch them."

"That's good," I said, as I truly loved the rabbits that lived in our yard. "What's an otterhound?" I asked. Was it half otter, half hound?

"Oh, otterhounds are wonderful dogs, but there aren't many of them. They are very smart, very friendly, and very, very playful. I've never seen one before Molly, but I can say she is one of the nicest dogs I've ever met. Molly's owner said her granddaughter loves to play with the puppies, and although Molly is very protective of them, she is gentle and passive around the little girl. That says a lot about her! And she is absolutely beautiful. She has long, floppy ears and hair that hangs over her eyes, and a tail that doesn't stop wagging. We'll pick up a book at the library this week and learn more about them. Border collies, of course, are wonderful dogs. I think it's a nice mix."

She scratched the pup under his chin. "He doesn't have a name yet. That will be up to you. Do you have any idea what you might like to call him?"

I knew exactly what I would call him, of course, for I had given it considerable thought. Having wanted a puppy for so long, I imagined him being full of energy, playful, and de-lightfully bold. I envisioned him running happily through the meadow, chasing butterflies and rolling through the thick green grass. But he would always be mindful of my presence and would never stray far from my side. It was as if he were as much a part of me as my breath and just as vital to my existence.

"Yes," I said without hesitation. "I want to call him Spirit."

"Spirit! Why, that's a perfect name," she said, cradling the puppy's head in her hands. "Welcome to our family, Spirit." She kissed him on the nose and hugged me around my neck. "Happy birthday, precious," she said. Then she made a fresh batch of pancakes and added extra butter and syrup, which I wolfed down in a matter of seconds.

"That was delicious," I said, although I hadn't tasted a single bite. I was much too excited about my birthday present to pay attention to food.

Mom smiled and shook her head as she cleared the table, and I sat on the floor with Spirit.

"It looks like it's going to be a very beautiful day." She gazed out the window. "Why don't you take your shower and get dressed so you and Spirit can go outside? Also, I'm quite sure Mrs. Robbins will stop by to wish you a happy birthday. It would be nice if you were dressed when she arrives."

"Okay, Mom. Will you keep Spirit company while I'm gone?" I picked up my pup and buried my face in his soft fur as he licked me once again.

"My pleasure," she said cheerfully as I handed him over to the safety of her arms.

I took a shower and got dressed in record time; I didn't want to be away from Spirit for more than a moment. After brushing my teeth and hair, I ran down the stairs singing, "I love you, Spirit! Oh yes, I do!" I jumped from the third step onto the floor and landed with a loud thud that rattled the house and startled Spirit, who began barking from the other room.

"Good heavens!" I heard someone cry out.

I ran into the kitchen to find Mrs. Robbins sitting at the table and a large gift box next to her on the floor. I was surprised by the size of the box and couldn't wait to open it, but not wanting to appear impolite, I pretended not to notice it.

"I'm very sorry, Mrs. Robbins. I didn't mean to startle you," I said sincerely.

"Yes, well...perhaps you should consider walking down the steps like a lady instead of jumping like a little heathen." She brushed a wayward strand of hair from her brow and sat stoically, awaiting another apology.

"Yes, ma'am. I really am sorry," I said as my mother leaned over and kissed my forehead.

Spirit had stopped barking and was trying to climb up my legs. His tailed wagged so hard that I thought he might turn himself inside out. I picked him up to introduce him to Mrs. Robbins, who seemed to be sizing him up. She held out one hand, which he sniffed before licking it. Her face softened, and a smile nearly appeared as she gently lifted him onto her ample lap.

"His name is Spirit," I offered.

"Spirit. Hmm. Seems like the right name," she said.

Spirit sat on her lap, but his behind didn't stop wagging. He sat up and placed his front paws on her chest as she pulled her face from his incessant licks.

"That's enough, Spirit," she said. She repositioned the pup so he was curled up in the folds of her skirt. He squirmed for a moment until she patted him behind his ears and whispered, "Spirit is a good dog. Yes, he's a very good dog."

Her voice startled me. I'd never heard her speak in such a gentle tone. Spirit responded instantly, overcome by the hypnotic drone of her voice. His head suddenly appeared quite heavy as it drooped and bobbed from side to side. His eyelids fluttered and closed for only a moment, and then they popped wide open again as he raised his head slightly and then dropped it down. His desire to discover his new surroundings weakened as he lay in complete submission in the voluminous fabric.

"Whoa," I blurted in amazement. "How'd you do that?" I didn't want to admit it, but I was a little bit jealous of how quickly he took to her, and I wanted to know her trick.

"Well, I suppose I've known many dogs in my lifetime. One learns quickly how to handle them."

My mother smirked and shook her head mechanically while keeping her eyes on the dishes in the sink.

"If your mother had suggested a different animal, I would never have allowed it. I've never had any interest in cats or rabbits or birds or, heaven forbid, those exotic rats that people seem to think are so cute these days. Disgusting creatures."

I wondered what exotic rats she was talking about when my mother turned toward me and whispered, "Ferrets."

"Oh," I said with a nod of thanks.

"But," Mrs. Robbins said, "it was fate that brought you and that dog together. It's almost uncanny when you think of it. I received a call out of the blue from my accountant, and he told me his otterhound was about to whelp. Frankly, the news of his dog could not have been of less interest to me. But I didn't have a moment to react before he was 'suggesting' that I might like to take one of the mutts off his hands. I couldn't believe my ears!

"I was just about to ask him if he'd lost his mind when he said, 'This is not a request, Myrtle. It's an opportunity for you to wipe a very dirty slate clean.'

"The nerve of that man!" she huffed. "As if I hadn't already paid that debt a million times over."

Mrs. Robbins' eyes narrowed as she continued to rant. "Stupid fool! I can't imagine what made him think he could squeeze another drop of blood out of me over something that never concerned him in the first place."

"That's enough, Myrtle," my mother said firmly.

Mrs. Robbins' lips locked shut as she fixed her gaze squarely on my mother. I wanted to become invisible, as there was no telling in which direction things might turn. Lacking the ability to disappear, I sat down on the floor as quietly as possible, keeping myself out of the potential line of fire.

Mrs. Robbins shifted her weight around in the chair, apparently searching for a more strategic position from which to strike. It seemed she had forgotten that Spirit was still on her lap, and he was thrust this way and that, tangled in the billows of her skirt. I felt very sorry for him; he clearly had no idea what was happening. He reminded me of a sailor adrift on a raft in stormy seas. I thought for a moment he was about to abandon ship when Mrs. Robbins wrapped her hands around him like a life preserver and pulled him to the safety of her bosom. She cleared her throat and looked down at the dog.

"Well," she began, "the pregnancy was quite unexpected and unappreciated. I can assure you of that much."

It was quiet for a moment. My mother turned from the dishes to cast a watchful eye on Myrtle, who was not yet finished with her story.

"You see," she said, shifting her attention to me, "Spirit's mother, Molly, is a purebred blue fairy otterhound with a very impressive bloodline. Her mother earned her Grand Championship title before she had her first litter, and her father was Best in Show at the Spring Conformation just two years ago. The otterhound is an old British breed and very rare. There are only about four hundred in the United States today. My accountant was about to start breeding Molly when they discovered she was already pregnant. You can imagine how devastated the family was."

Mother turned back to her window as Mrs. Robbins looked down at Spirit, grave disappointment written all over her face.

"And then to find out that the father was a common mongrel, of all things!" She expelled another loud huff from her lips, and she shook her head in seeming disgust. "It was quite a blow to everyone," she said, far too seriously, and muttered, "Mmm...mmm...mmm." She shook her head, apparently waiting for my mother to turn around.

But Mother's gaze was fixed on the path just outside the kitchen window that travelled over the small stream and through the alley of giant elms that led to the front gate and freedom from Lindenwood.

Mrs. Robbins, who was not one to be ignored, cleared her throat several times until she began to cough while my mother waited until there was silence, never turning from the window.

"As I understand it," my mother said, "the father is a border collie, which makes Spirit half otterhound and half border collie."

"Ha! Border collies can hardly be considered a breed. They're nothing more than tramps who run wherever they please. I suspect this one sneaked onto the property at night when no one knew he was prowling around. It's the only way he would have gotten near such exquisite stock. Poor Molly! She's ruined forever, of course, as are her owners. No serious breeder would consider her now." Mrs. Robbins raised one eyebrow and stared at Spirit as if she were examining him for fleas.

"Anyway, there are no pedigrees for mutts; I can assure you of that much. And that is what makes the fateful pregnancy a complete disaster."

Wiping her hands on a kitchen towel, my mother turned slowly with eyes ablaze and faced her adversary. This time, it was Mrs. Robbins' turn to be aloof, and she focused all her attention on pitying Molly's poor owners while ignoring my mother's gaze. As my eyes darted back and forth between the two, I suddenly knew I was the only one who could disarm the ticking bomb that was about to explode. My mother took a deep breath. I feared it was already too late to divert the inevitable.

"What's a pedigree?" I asked much too loudly.

Mrs. Robbins looked at me as though I'd just walked into the room, and my mother stood guard; her hands planted squarely on her hips.

"It's an official ancestral chart that shows who is in the animal's family tree to prove the line is pure and from good stock," she said to me while trading stares with my mother. "But your dog doesn't qualify, so it's not something you need to concern yourself with."

My mother put down the kitchen towel she'd been holding in one hand as she stepped toward Mrs. Robbins. Her left cheek throbbed as she clenched her teeth. This was not a good sign. I held my breath, helpless against whatever was about to come. My eyes pleaded with my mom to stay calm, and I was hopeful when she glanced at me before standing in front of Mrs. Robbins.

"It is nothing more than a piece of paper that is completely worthless to people who love their dogs just the way they are," she said calmly. She wrapped her hands around Spirit's belly and removed him from his snug spot on Mrs. Robbins' lap. Then she lifted him above her head as his limp puppy legs dangled lifelessly in the air. She gave him a little shake, pulled him close, buried her face in his soft fur, and took a whiff of sweet puppy breath before giving him a kiss. "And that's just the way we love you, little one!"

Spirit's ear hung over my mother's nose as she nuzzled him. He looked like a beanbag dog as his legs dangled on either side of her hand. She passed him back to Mrs. Robbins, who was noticeably reluctant to receive the dog this time. I felt very sorry for him. They were treating Spirit more like a prop than a pup, and I hoped he wasn't offended. The exchange was extremely awkward, and I was about to grab Spirit away from the two of them when Mrs. Robbins took the dog from my mother's outstretched hand.

"We thank you for permitting this perfect new addition to our little family, Myrtle," she said.

The two women traded icy stares. Mother turned away from her and walked back to her spot at the sink. Mrs. Robbins continued to glare at my mother's back with her eyebrows raised and nostrils flared. Spirit looked quite uncomfortable as she held him in a suspended pose that kept his rear end from fully squatting into the soft ripples of her skirt. He must have sensed the tension between my mother and Mrs. Robbins, as he didn't budge or make a single sound.

The silence was making me sick to my stomach, and I thought I might throw up when my mother turned and said, "Spirit is our dog and our responsibility. So you have absolutely nothing to concern yourself with. My perfect daughter will ensure her equally perfect pup will be loved and well cared for. You won't even know he's here." She glanced at me for affirmation. "Isn't that right, dear?"

The room was spinning, and my heart was beating so loudly that it sounded as if drums were pounding in my head. All I wanted was for this awkwardness to be over. I couldn't understand how everyone's mood had changed so drastically, but I knew it was up to me to get things back in order.

I looked at Mrs. Robbins with wide eyes and an assuring grin. "Oh yes, Mrs. Robbins, I'll take very good care of him. I promise!"

I waited for a sign that the spell had been broken, but Mrs. Robbins' eyes remained fixed on my mother, who was standing her ground. I knew my mother had been rude, but I couldn't tell if Mrs. Robbins was hurt, angry, or both. I didn't want her to be anything but happy. I ran over to her and gave her a big hug around the neck. "Thank you so, so much for letting me have my wonderful Spirit," I said, my words smothered in her shoulder. "I'll take good care of him. And I'll love him forever."

Mrs. Robbins loosened her grip on Spirit, and he slid happily into her lap. She patted my back with one hand as I held my pose.

She finally said, "That's quite enough, dear."

I stepped back with a goofy smile on my face. Her face remained hardened as she turned her attention to the dog, who had rolled just enough to get his belly rubbed.

"Well, I suppose the good news is that you like him," Mrs. Robbins said, still not cracking a smile. "It would be nothing less than a disaster otherwise. I can't give a single thought to the ramifications of taking him back to my accountant, especially under the circumstances. Good heavens!"

My mother's eyes narrowed, and her lips pursed tightly as she threatened Mrs. Robbins with her gaze. I held on to my goofy smile for dear life but dared not look at either woman.

"Anyway," she said, "you really have nothing to thank me for. It was your mother's idea, certainly not mine. I just happened to be obligated to my accountant at the time. That's the way things sometimes go."

It wasn't the positive response I was hoping for, but the ice seemed to have been broken. I was breathing a bit more easily.

She added, "At any rate I'm sure Spirit will learn the rules quickly enough, and when he does, he will be welcome around the house."

By "around the house," Mrs. Robbins meant the cottage we lived in and the sixty-five acres that surrounded it. I don't believe her own very grand old home was included in this assessment, as she rarely welcomed humans into her residence, let alone a dog.

Of course, there were more than enough places for him to roam without ever venturing near the main house. In addition to the cottage, there were two large barns, an old mill, a stable, and a carriage house that was situated above a four-car garage where three classic automobiles in mint condition were parked alongside Mother's old Honda Civic. The carriage house, which was fully furnished, had never seen a single visitor, although it was maintained as though the occupants were expected to return at any moment. The same was true of the stable; hay was strewn about the stalls, and troughs were replenished with fresh water daily, just in case a few horses showed up. I asked my mother why Mrs. Robbins never had any visitors,   even though she had plenty of places where they could stay.

She just said, "I don't know, dear. It's been this way since the day I moved in."

I was never very clear as to how all that came about, as my mother never discussed how she wound up at Lindenwood. But one day, when she'd gone into town to run errands, Mrs. Robbins told me that my grandparents were the poorest people in the town of Grace Falls, and quite possibly, the entire state of Pennsylvania. They struggled just to put food on the table and keep a roof over their heads. She said they were older when my mother was born and were in poor health for years. My mother was ten years old when her parents died of pneumonia. Having never taken time to prepare a last will and testament, and without any known living relatives, their passing left my mother in a very desperate state, as she was immediately sent to the county orphanage. The whole town knew about my mother's sad situation, and everyone felt very badly for her, but no one knew what to do. Several people from the church who were particularly concerned about her welfare called Mrs. Robbins and asked her to help. There was no other choice, of course, so Mrs. Robbins agreed. Without giving it a second thought, she plucked my mother from the hands of a dreadful fate and treated her as her own. After that, the entire town praised Mrs. Robbins for her altruism, and everyone was very happy for the little orphan who was now a princess.

"Why hasn't my mother told me any of this?" I asked. It was clear to me that Mrs. Robbins had been extraordinarily kind to my mother and that the story had a very happy ending.

She said that perhaps talking about her parents made her very sad, since she lost them at such an early age. "Or," she once suggested, "she might be painfully embarrassed by the fact that they were so devastatingly poor. I'm sure she'll share this with you one day, in her own way, when she's ready. But until she does, let's keep this our little secret. After all, we don't want to upset or embarrass her over things that are in the past now, do we?"

I thought Mrs. Robbins made an excellent point, as I never wanted to hurt my mother in any way. But the much bigger reason for not telling her about my conversation with Mrs. Robbins was that I enjoyed keeping a secret. It made me feel important and, in this case, better connected to Mrs. Robbins than my mother was. Her relationship was one of a long-term employee, while mine felt like it was becoming more personal. I wondered if perhaps she could sense things about me that my mother had yet to discover or if she might be testing me to see if I could be trusted. Either way, I didn't want to disappoint her. So I kept her story safe within.

I believed that Mrs. Robbins had taken my mom in when she had nowhere else to go, and I wished she would be kinder toward her or at least more grateful. Especially on this day, when it seemed that everything we had we owed to Mrs. Robbins. And now we had her to thank for Spirit as well.

"So," Mrs. Robbins said after a moment, "today is your birthday!"

I was smiling ear to ear, as I was certain a present was coming my way.

"Yes, it is!"

"Well, happy birthday, Lily," she said as she slid the big box toward me.

"Oh wow! Is that for me?" I pretended I had just noticed it, which made me feel a little foolish. But my mother laughed.

"Yes, of course it is," Mrs. Robbins said. "But it's also for Spirit."

I tore off the ribbon and paper to expose a cardboard box that was heavily taped on the top and bottom. I tried to tear the tape but had no luck, so my mother grabbed a pair of scissors from the drawer.

"I've got it," she said. And with one swipe, the top of the box was open.

Inside was blue and yellow tissue paper that had been carefully crumpled to hide the contents underneath. I pulled all the paper out of the box and was surprised to find three more boxes that were also wrapped up and tied with ribbons and bows. By this time, Spirit had become tired of sitting on Mrs. Robbins' lap and wanted to get in on the action. She lowered him onto the floor as he growled at the paper and then grabbed onto one of the ribbons and gave it a mighty shake. Mrs. Robbins took hold of the ribbon and played a game of tug-of-war with him. Mother and I laughed at his bravado. When he grew tired of the tugging game, he lunged at the paper and ripped it to pieces, flipping it up in the air and rolling over it.

"Spirit," I said, giggling, "you're the funniest dog ever!"

The boxes that were inside the big box were things that Spirit needed as a permanent resident of our household—two dog bowls, one for food and one for water; a collar with a leash already attached; a bag of Puppy Chow; and a poop scoop.

"Oh, thank you, Mrs. Robbins! That was so thoughtful of you. I almost forgot that we had to feed him."

"And walk him," my mother added.

"I'll walk him every day."

Mrs. Robbins said there was another present in the big box, which turned out to be under even more blue and yellow tissue paper. I reached in and pulled out a beautiful quilted dog bed that Mrs. Robbins "paid a pretty dollar" to have made.

"He'll need a place to sleep that's all his own," she said.

I was secretly hoping he could sleep with me, but I said cheerfully, "It's beautiful, Mrs. Robbins. Thank you so, so much!"

"You're quite welcome. But, you know, this is Spirit's first night away from his mother. Up until now he's always slept by her side. It will take him a day or two to get used to sleeping alone."

"He could sleep in my bed," I suggested quickly, thinking this was the perfect time to make the offer.

My mother chuckled. "I'm afraid not, Lily," she said. "Spirit needs to know that even when he's alone, we will always come back. And he'll be even happier to see you when he wakes up if he had a chance to miss you. How else will he be able to survive on the days when you're in school?"

That made sense to me. After all, I didn't want him to ever be sad. And the thought of him happily greeting me after school was something I wanted very badly.

"But isn't he going to be lonely in his own bed without his mother or me beside him?"

Mrs. Robbins was the one who was prepared for this question. "Not with this!"

She reached in the box and pulled out one last gift. It was a small pillow that was made from the same quilted fabric as the dog bed, but it looked more like something that belonged to a doll.

He's never going to put his head on that, I thought. How would this new surprise solve Spirit's sleeping problems?

Mrs. Robbins lifted a flap in the back of the pillow and turned a small knob as the pillow started ticking. "Listen," she said as she held it to my ear.

"It's a clock!" I exclaimed, having no idea what her plan might be.

"That's right," said Mrs. Robbins. "If you put the clock pillow in the bed with Spirit, he will think it is his mother's heartbeat. It will soothe him until he is able to fall asleep. He might cry when you first put him to bed, but the clock will help. It's an old trick my mother taught me with my first dog, and it's worked with every pup I had since."

I was sceptical and certain that allowing Spirit to sleep in my bed would be a much better solution. But I gave Mrs. Robbins a big hug and thanked her for her thoughtfulness.

It wasn't long after I opened her gifts that Mrs. Robbins stood to leave.

"Spirit and I could walk you to the house," I offered cheerfully.

"That won't be necessary, dear. I found my way here; I can find my way back."

Mother huffed and shook her head. I was a little bit hurt, but I didn't want my mom to know, so I gave Mrs. Robbins another hug and thanked her again for the gifts. My mother shut the door behind Mrs. Robbins as soon as she stepped out and then muttered something under her breath. I couldn't hear what she said, but I suspected it wasn't complimentary.

"How about if the three of us play awhile in the yard?" she suggested.

I was quick to answer yes.

It was a picture-perfect day, and the sun shone brightly through the trees as we played with Spirit for hours. He was quite worn out when lunchtime rolled around. We fed him from his new bowls and then put him in his quilted bed for a nap. I laid down on the floor next to him to keep him company, but he was out like a light before I knew it. I leaned closer to his face to smell his sweet puppy breath as he dozed.

"Let's leave him alone for a bit and have our lunch outside," Mom suggested.

I got up as quietly as possible and tiptoed to the door, careful not to disturb my precious Spirit.

CHAPTER 4

AS SPIRIT SLEEPS

M other took a big quilted blanket outside and spread it under the elm tree that stood near the kitchen door. "We can hear him from here," she said, with a smile. Then we settled beneath the tree as a light breeze carried the scent of lilacs and hyacinth in the air.

"Can we plant a vegetable garden this year?" I asked out of the blue.

"You mean aside from Myrtle's garden?"

Myrtle's was a very large garden situated in an area that couldn't be seen from the main house but was in clear view from the cottage. It yielded an abundant crop each year of corn, carrots, cucumbers, cauliflower, and squash that was far more than the three mouths living on the estate could eat. My mother would stash bushels of vegetables away in the barn for the people who worked on the property to take home for their families. It was a covert operation that had to be kept secret from Mrs. Robbins, who was against any kind of charity and was particularly opposed to giving things away to people she already employed. Had she gotten wind of my mother's underground mission, she might have plowed over the garden and fired all the workers rather than give them food that would otherwise go to waste.

"I think it would be fun to have a small garden of our own that we could take care of together. We could plant things like cherry tomatoes. I love cherry tomatoes! And maybe some green beans."

"Well...the fun is often in the planning. It's the planting that can be a chore. But it's a good idea," she said, without committing. Then she asked, "Don't you like Myrtle's vegetables?"

"It's not that," I said. "I guess it would just be nice to have a garden that was all our own." I glanced around the property that belonged to Mrs. Robbins, knowing that the garden wouldn't be ours, even if we were the ones who planted it. "We could share our vegetables with Mrs. Robbins. She might like that. And we could add some to the ones you give to the workers. I'm sure that would make them happy."

My mother sat up and looked around nervously. "Shh!" she whispered. "You must never let Myrtle know about that. Promise me, Lily; it's very important."

"I know," I said. "I just thought that—"

She frowned as she held her finger to her lips and shook her head.

"Okay," I said. And another secret was safe with me.

My mother's eyes surveyed the property in search of an ideal spot for the garden. "Let's clear an area next to the big garden. The soil is perfect there, and it will be easy to add an extra row or two," she reasoned.

"Do you think it will be okay with Mrs. Robbins?"

"She'll never even know it's there," she said.

Mother's eyes twinkled as she spread our lunches on the blanket. It was clear to me that she had something more than a picnic up her sleeve.

"Did you know," she asked with a playful smile, "that Mira's mother and grandmother were great gardeners?"

"Is that so?" I said, happily playing along.

"Oh yes," she began excitedly. "And outstanding cooks as well. Every meal was made from the delicious fruits and vegetables that were picked each day from their garden. The Two were intuitively aware of the generosity and wisdom of Mother Nature, and they treated her precious resources with profound respect and appreciation. And being a good and faithful Mother, she reciprocated with an overflowing bounty of nutritious food that nurtured their bodies as well as their souls."

I took a bite of my PB and J as I waited for her story to unfold.

"The Two were busy from dusk until dawn, but they were never tired of their chores. They gave each one an equal measure of love, care, and attention. Using their gifts for the common good was as natural as breathing for Mira's family, and they delighted in the joy that their contributions brought to those who were less fortunate or in a season of need. Amazingly, everything they put their hands and hearts to was multiplied far beyond their needs. This gift was known as the miracle of provision, and it was available to anyone who relied upon the wisdom and power of the One for all things. For He was abundant in His provision, and they, in turn, gave joyfully to others." My mother paused as she glanced at the abundance all around her. A sadness appeared in her eyes that looked like regret; her voice was somber when she spoke again.

"Most of the world had stopped trusting in the One. Some questioned His existence, while others questioned His motivations. Still others questioned why they needed Him at all. Those were the ones who believed the Enemy's lies that they were superior to others and entitled to whatever they cared to take. Even if they had no right to it." She shook her head as she surveyed all that was around her.

"But the Enemy's lie took away more than it gave, and many people had to strive very hard every single day for things they didn't need, sacrificing time that could have been spent with those who loved them for the promise of things that had no value at all."

The sorrow I heard in my mother's voice suddenly filled me with immeasurable despair. I thought for a moment I might be swallowed by my helplessness. I couldn't shake the feeling that the entire world was about to explode into a zillion pieces while I sat frozen in self-imposed fear. It wasn't the first time this had happened, and my mother was quick to recognize the signs of anxiety that were about to consume me. As usual she came to my rescue just in the nick of time.

"But that was not the case with Mira's family," she chortled in a cartoon voice. "Heaven's no! Why, their very existence created a powerful, positive energy that benefited every living thing and generated unprecedented kindness and immeasurable love."

I snapped back to life at the sound of her bright, animated voice and took a deep, cleansing breath to expel the bad air from my lungs.

"Go on," I said with a big grin.

Mother smiled but kept her eye on me as she continued.

"The Two were highly regarded for their culinary skills, but their gifts extended far beyond those found in their kitchen, for they were known both far and wide as the most accomplished and talented seamstresses who ever lived. Anyone and everyone from Everywhere, Anywhere, and Beyond longed for the privilege to own a mere swatch of cloth that was created by the Two."

My ears perked up as I heard the unspoken word "fashion" being uttered. I was secretly hoping that there was a surprise in store that included a drastic change to my wardrobe. This was just wishful thinking, of course, as the subject of my wardrobe had never come up and hadn't seemed very important until recently. But I had begun to feel self-conscious about my clothes, as they were noticeably different than those of the popular kids at school. Theirs were made by famous designers and were far more expensive than the no-name brands I wore. Of course, that was how you knew they were popular. You had to have the right clothes to be part of the in crowd, as it was the first step in even being noticed. Which, I never was or would be, if my wardrobe didn't change.

Not that I wasn't grateful for the clothes I had. They were very nice in many ways. But they were more my mother's taste than my own, and of course, they fit into our very limited budget.

Many times, when we went shopping, Mom would steer me clear of things she wasn't fond of or couldn't afford by saying, "That color's not right for you," or "You'll be tired of that before we get out of the store."

I never knew why I had to get what she wanted instead of what I wanted. But I didn't want to offend or upset her, so I did my best to be satisfied with what I'd been given. Still I wished she would ask me if there was something I'd like better. I was secretly hoping she was leading up to that now.

"Everyone marveled at the clothing they made, as they were not only wonderful to look at, but they were delightful to wear. Folks oohed and ahhed when they put on something made by the Two.

"Many had been heard to say, 'I don't ever want to wear anything else,' and some, it turns out, never did.

"For the true magic of anything made by the Two was in its ability to last forever yet always look brand new. The secret to this phenomenon was in the combination of two enormously creative spirits who were equally blessed with highly practical minds. Although they were capable of creating the next craze in fashion, they knew that fashion would always go out of style and was quickly replaced. So, they stuck with the formula that worked for centuries by focusing on function, form, and comfort as they set out to poke through piles of plains, plaids, and patterns, picking just the right materials for the best garment ever made and making it last forever."

I squinted as I looked toward the sun and watched the clouds pass under the boughs of the great tree. My thoughts had begun to wander, which did not go unnoticed by my mother, who cleared her throat to get my attention. "Sorry," I said mechanically, and she meandered on.

"Another gift of the miraculous Two was their sensitivity to things that most people take for granted or pay absolutely no attention to.

"'Everyone is happier when they have a place where they belong,' Grammy would say. They believed this was true of all things, especially those that coexisted in one's home."

I was trying hard to look as though I was paying attention, but something unsettling had been churning around in my head. I couldn't put my finger on what it was, but it prevented me from processing my mother's words.

"This, for instance," I thought I heard her say, "was the way the Two dealt with the family's clothes."

Then I drifted back to the clouds as the still unidentified, nagging thought gnawed its way through the back of my brain.

"Shirts, shorts, skirts, slacks, and shoes were each assigned their own space in a closet or drawer, which, amazingly enough, added to their immeasurable comfort. This happens because everything has an energy that is either positive or negative. And when things are surrounded by things they are most complimented by, they transmit positive energy that is experienced by everyone and everything around them.

"Think about that for a moment," she commanded.

I blinked several times to refocus before turning my gaze back to her.

"Creating a space where everything belonged was a very wise and thoughtful thing to do."

"Wait a minute," I said as the troublesome notion revealed itself. "They wore the same clothes all the time? How is that possible?" I didn't know where the story was going, but it was clear that it was not leading up to a new wardrobe for me. "Who would want to wear the same clothes forever? I mean...seriously! You'd be bored stiff just getting dressed every day." My irrational anger thumped hard in my chest, and my mouth was suddenly as dry as a bone.

"Well…I'm afraid I don't know what to say." My mother handed me a glass of lemonade. "But you've made a very good point. I can see that wearing the same clothes every day might not be very exciting."

"Humph! That's an understatement," I huffed.

"Yes, but if you can stay with me for just a moment, I think I can redeem the story."

I shifted back to a cross-legged position and waited with a smug look still plastered on my face.

"Having a place where clothes, furniture, pots, pans, and all things useful belonged kept everyone happy and comfortable in the not-too-big-not-too-small house on the hill," she finally began. "Some things stayed in the house forever, while others were passed on to folks from Anywhere, Everywhere, and Beyond who needed them more than Mira's family did. When that time came, they were thanked for their long and faithful service then placed in the hands of a new, loving family who welcomed them into their home with extraordinary joy."

"But what about the clothes?" I asked arrogantly as I cross-examined my mother. "Did Mira get new clothes or not?" I was losing my patience and was certain she could never answer my question without retracting her original statement.

"Yes, dear." She chuckled. "She got new clothes."

I waited.

"But never more than she needed."

Bingo! I thought as I braced for the lesson that was bound to follow.

"Mira's mother and grandmother were very considerate of all things, not just people. Naturally they loved Mira with all their hearts and wanted her to be happy and, above all else, healthy. But they knew that love is not measured in possessions. More of something, especially when it is not used or needed, is not only wasteful, it is most disrespectful. So, when Mira outgrew a piece of clothing either in size or in taste, the old was removed from its place and replaced with the new."

That's reasonable, I thought, careful not to give away my approval.

"But there was never more put back than what was taken. So a single pair of new pants would be neatly placed in the space that the original pair occupied. One pair of pants would never be replaced by two, as that would create an overcrowded condition for all the clothing, and that would never do. It would soon result in a pile of sad, unused, and terribly uncomfortable clothing spilling out of drawers or falling from their hangers, lying in crumpled heaps on the floor, where they would be overlooked or purposely ignored. How very sad for the clothing who wanted nothing more than to be useful." She wore a sorrowful look. "You can see how that could create quite a problem, right?"

I suddenly wished I had picked up my clothes from my bedroom floor instead of allowing her to do it.

"Yes, I see," I muttered.

"Good," she exclaimed more cheerfully than I believed was warranted. "Then there's just one more point that needs to be made."

Oh, give it up! I said in desperation—but not out loud, of course.

"Everything had a purpose and a place in Mira's not-too-big-not-too-small house because in that way, everything was part of her perfect family.

"'Love and care for all things,' Mira's father would say, 'giving thanks to the One Who Provides, for everything we have comes from Him.'"

I was about to ask her about the One Who Provides, but my tolerance for lessons was running low, so I decided to leave it for another time. Anyway, it was my birthday! And I wanted to play with my dog.

"Shouldn't we check on Spirit?" I asked, ensuring the story would end for the time being.

"Absolutely," she replied agreeably. "You go on inside. I'll take care of this."

She gathered up the paper plates, napkins, and leftovers as I ran into the house, where I found Spirit squatting near his bed, a yellow stream trickling behind him.

"Spirit!" I cried as Mother dropped everything and ran toward the door. Spirit was not quite finished when she burst into the kitchen.

"Oh," she sighed with relief. "I guess I forgot about this part." She laughed and then rolled her eyes. "We have to potty train him," she said.

"Potty train him?" An image of him sitting on a toilet passed through my mind. "How are we supposed to do that?"

"Well, the first thing we have to do is clean up this mess." She handed Spirit to me, and I sneered at the pee that was dripping from his back paws. "Hold on, I'll get some paper towels." She stepped over the stream to get to the sink while both Spirit and I stood suspended in space.

I was much less disgusted after she wiped his wet paws with damp towels, although my expression hadn't changed, as the scent of fresh urine wafted through the air.

"Yuck!" I blurted.

"Take Spirit outside for a while. I think he needs to get the smell of grass, so he knows where his bathroom is."

I was happy to get out of the kitchen, and I'm sure Spirit was as well. My mother joined us after cleaning up and explained that the best way to train Spirit not to go in the house was to get him on a schedule of going outside.

"He's just a puppy, so he's bound to have accidents, but a dog's instinct is to do their business outside. If we are very diligent about a bathroom routine, it shouldn't take him long before he lets us know when he needs to go out. In the meantime, I think we'll confine him to the laundry room and make sure there are plenty of newspapers for him to squat on. And during the day, we'll keep the door open, so he has fresh air and can get a good whiff of the lovely lawn that's waiting for him."

I was upset by this thought. "Does that mean he can't go in other parts of the house?"

"Oh no," she explained. "He'll go wherever we go. But when we're busy or have someplace to go, he'll have a nice spot that's all his where we won't have to worry about him getting into trouble."

I was relieved and very agreeable to the arrangement. I liked the idea of Spirit having his own space, and the laundry room was the perfect spot. It was located just off the kitchen, which was where we spent most of our time. The door that led outside from the laundry room was almost never used, as it emptied into the side yard, where there was no path. My mother used to call it the "door to nowhere" and often placed things in front of it that prevented it from being easily opened.

"We'll have to take the folding table from the room, but that won't be a big deal. I'll just fold the laundry on the kitchen table." She looked lovingly at Spirit. "Please keep this minor inconvenience in my mind whenever you're thinking of tinkling in the house instead of in the yard," she told him sarcastically.

He stared up at her with wide eyes as if to say, "Yes, ma'am," and then wiggled his way to her bare feet before rolling over on his back.

"He wants a belly rub." She leaned down to tickle his pink little tummy; and we all sat together in the grass as Spirit tugged on the strings of our hearts.

CHAPTER 5

NO WAY TO END A DAY

The day flew by quickly, and soon it was time to get myself and Spirit ready for bed. I was still hoping that Spirit would be allowed to sleep in my room, but Mother insisted that he stay downstairs so as not to awaken me through the night. I considered protesting but knew it would be futile. Besides, I was too overcome by the joy of a perfect day to waste a single breath on anything but gratitude. I stood before the mirror in my favorite pink and gray pajamas watching my mother as she brushed my hair. This had been part of our nightly routine for as long as I could remember, mostly because my hair drove my mother a little crazy.

"This hair has a mind of its own," she would say after another useless attempt to keep the wispy strands from assaulting my face.

She tried everything from barrettes to gel to very short cuts, but nothing could tame my unruly mousey-brown mane. It didn't help that the hair on the back of my head had several stubborn cowlicks that made it curly, while the hair on the sides was very fine and perfectly straight. To anyone else it would have been a losing battle. But to my mother, it was just something else she had to deal with.

"I think if we keep it no longer than shoulder length and comb the curls out every night, we might be able to train it to behave." Her plan hadn't worked so far.

"Mommy," I began as she tackled the knots and tangles in my hair, "do you think Daddy would have loved Spirit as much as we do?"

The hairbrush halted halfway through my cowlicks, and a tiny gasp passed through my mother's lips just before she stopped breathing.

"I mean, he loved dogs, right? You said he was always bringing home strays and taking care of them until he found them good homes. So, he must have loved them."

"Oh my, yes," she said, after taking a deep breath. "Nothing could be truer of your father. He loved all animals, but he had an affinity for dogs, especially those in need of a home."

My face lit up as the longing in my heart pleaded for more. I loved my mother's stories of the compassionate, selfless man who was tragically lost while serving his country before I was born. Her grand accounts of my father's unparalleled love and kindness for the earth and everything in it filled me with joy. I wanted to be just like the man I'd never met. I waited for my mother's words to summon the spirit of one who was too good to be true, and fill my heart with his presence.

"He never turned away a single stray," she said. "He cared for them as if they were his own while he searched high and low for the perfect family who was meant to be theirs alone. When a match was found, he took them to their forever home, where they lived happily ever after."

My eyes sparkled with hope.

"So," she said, "the answer to your question is…yes! Yes, darling. He would have loved Spirit with all his heart. Just as he loved you."

My smile was ear to ear as she kissed the top of my head and turned me toward my bed. It had been a long day, and my body was ready for sleep. But the smell of the freshly laundered linens awakened my senses, and the crisp white cotton beckoned me to make snow angels in the sheets as my mother shook her head.

"Where does all that energy come from?" she asked as she swept away the angels and straightened up the sheets.

I wiggled under the covers, so she could tuck me in. But I was not yet ready for sleep.

"Mom," I began, propped up on one elbow, "you know how you always say that Daddy is in heaven and his spirit watches over us every day?" She smiled and gave me a nod. "Well, I was just thinking…if he wants to be with us as much as we want to be with him, maybe he decided to reincarnate and come back as a dog."

The shock that registered on my mother's face was off the charts, and she stood frozen in place with her eyes opened wide. There was no question that this was the most imaginative thought I'd had in my eleven years, and it turned everything that had always been true upside down. It was as if in a split second we supernaturally switched roles and she was the one who searched for logic and reason while I floated carelessly on a cloud of impossibility.

"*Wow!*" she finally exclaimed more loudly than warranted. "Wouldn't that be something?" Her head bobbed up and down as if it was on a spring while I continued to hold on to my lifeline of irrational thinking.

"It's a very interesting idea, Lily," she offered, while I remained convicted that I'd just uncovered a great mystery of life. "Really!" she continued unconvincingly. "I absolutely wouldn't have thought of that one myself. Not in a million years!"

The fact that my mother was stumbling over her words somehow gave me hope. What if my idea had come from a source far greater than either my mother or me? What if I'd just been given a key to a door in the universe that held the secret to eternal life? What if what I thought, was true…and my father was Spirit?

"Honey," my mother began, "I know this isn't what you want to hear. But the truth is…people don't come back after they're gone. We've talked about this, right? I mean… we've talked about life and death, haven't we?"

No…we never talked about life and death. Or about anything that truly mattered. I had an unspoken understanding of what she believed in, but that didn't mean I agreed with her. It just meant that I didn't want to disagree out loud.

"I mean, it's very, very sad," she said to my blank stare. "But it's something we have to accept. There is no such thing as reincarnation. People die, and they don't come back. They don't come back as snails or animals or even other people. They just don't. Death is a part of life, and we have no control over it. It's simply not up to us when someone will die, and we don't understand why or how it happens. It just happens."

My heart pounded violently inside of my chest. I wanted to scream in protest and make everything she said disappear. And...I wanted her to disappear, too.

"The best we can do is be grateful for the time they were here on earth," she offered feebly, "and be thankful for the love they left behind."

My mind was a maelstrom of emotions and fear that threated to burst inside of my brain, and I was helpless against the powerful force that was about to explode.

"But that's not fair!" I erupted. "I never had a chance even to meet him, so how am I supposed to be grateful? How do I give thanks for something I never knew?" My fists pounded the bed as tears filled my eyes. "*Argh!*" I shouted into my pillow. "*It stinks!*" I lifted my head and spoke to the ceiling, avoiding my mother. "Just because you got to love him doesn't mean I did."

My mind was not capable of controlling my fear as spirits of rejection and abandonment soon took hold of my brain. I wallowed in self-pity as remorse and regret for the words I'd just spoken overwhelmed and convicted me of the unforgivable sin of breaking my mother's heart.

"It's your fault he's not here," the voice in my head said as guilt and despair swallowed up everything that was left of my spirit.

I needed my mother now more than ever, but I didn't have the courage to face her. I wished I could erase everything that just happened and restore my life to the moment before I stepped out of my comfort zone and ventured into the realm of the impossible. I didn't belong in my mother's creative world. That was her turf, not mine. And I made a vow to never again imagine more than I could grasp.

But my immediate problem was that dying seemed like a more acceptable alternative than facing my mother. I laid perfectly still with my head buried in my very damp pillow when I felt my mother's hand glide gently across the small of my back. Every rigid muscle in my body melted by her touch as the walls I'd built around my heart came crashing down.

"Lily," she said, just above a whisper. "Lily," she repeated. "Honey, I'm so sorry."

I tossed the pillow onto the floor, spun around, and threw myself into her arms as she rocked me back and forth.

"I'm sorry, Mommy! I'm so sorry! I didn't mean it," I confessed.

"Shh," she quieted me as we continued swaying. "It's okay. I get it. I do."

We stayed in that position until I knew it was safe to look at her and she at me. Then I unwrapped my arms from around her neck and sat with my back against the pillows as she wiped the tears that were still on my face.

"The thing is," she said, brushing strands of hair from my eyes, "I know that you feel your dad's love every day. I know you do. If you didn't, you wouldn't be able to miss him."

I held on to her words for dear life.

"Love is not something that lives in the wind, Lily. It isn't here one day and gone the next. Real love exists in the very air that we breathe. It fills us up and gives us life. The air never goes away, even if people do."

My heart leapt; I wanted desperately to believe what she said was true.

"Close your eyes, honey," she instructed as she held my hand. "Now pretend that your lungs are a single red balloon that you are filling up with air. Then take a deep, deep breath, and hold on to it for a moment."

I did just as she said. Closing my eyes, I imagined my lungs as one big balloon that expanded as my breath poured into it. Holding on to the air, I felt the balloon begin to pulsate, as if it had its own heartbeat. The feeling wasn't uncomfortable, as I'd expected it would be; instead it felt as if new life was inside of me. I welcomed this feeling and held on to it for as long as I could. Then I released the air very slowly until every breath was expelled. I kept my eyes closed until my lungs functioned normally again.

"That was Daddy!" I stated.

This undeniable truth brought an awareness that my father's presence was as close as my breathing, and it filled every cell and fiber within me. I looked at my mother with awe and smiled as I wiped the tears from her eyes. The air was unquestionably lighter all around me, and I wanted to lie awake all night just to breathe it in. I scooted down under the covers to get ready for sleep, but my mind refused to cooperate.

"Why don't we have any pictures of him?" I asked as my mom reached to turn out the light.

She sighed as she pulled her hand away from the switch and sat down in the chair next to my bed.

"I don't know," she replied as she made herself comfortable. "He was in the army when we met, and it seemed as if he was always away on one assignment or another, so we didn't want to waste a single moment of the time we were given. When I think about it, I doubt that we gave any thought at all to taking pictures. Of course,"—she sniggered—"things might have been different if we'd had a camera."

"Minor point," I said as she nodded and smiled.

My mother's stories of my father were like a romance novel of a courageous young soldier whose love for his country was an overpowering force in his life. She described him many times as a hero who was driven by a warrior's spirit that was only satisfied by the relentless pursuit of freedom for those who were unable to fight for themselves. As a true champion for the underprivileged and downtrodden, he left the comfort of home to travel to sundrenched deserts where men were blinded by powerful sandstorms and many fell victim to the intense heat that surrounded them. His heart beat to help others. He never quit, and he never gave up hope as he continued to return again and again to the battleground until one day when he didn't come home. My mother's stories about my father were epic and often beyond my comprehension. But I soaked every one of them in and embraced her memories as if they were my own. To me he was bigger than life, and no one in my eyes could ever live up to the man who sacrificed his life for others.

It seems strange now, but I had never asked my mother for a detailed physical description of my father. I don't know why. I certainly never suspected that she had intentionally withheld this information from me. But the need to know him overwhelmed me, and my mother knew there was no escaping the task she had avoided until now.

"Do you want me to paint a picture for you?" she asked.

"Oh yes, please!"

She closed her eyes as her nostrils flared to take in a deep breath. "You don't deserve this," she whispered as the air left her lips.

I asked her what she'd meant by that, but she brushed me off and pulled her chair closer to me. She sat low in the seat, her legs stretched out on the bed, arms folded across her chest. I thought she was ready to begin when she wiggled around again, this time with a deeply furrowed brow. It looked like she was trying to escape from a straitjacket, and an eternity passed before she finally leaned back into the chair, bowed her head, and took one more deep breath. "You'll have to close those big brown eyes," she instructed.

"Breathe deeply, and let go of all your thoughts. Empty your mind of everything. Just pretend it is a blank canvas, and my words are the strokes of a paintbrush."

My eyes were shut tight, and I tried hard to follow her directions.

"Don't forget to breathe," I heard her say, and I felt my face soften and my body relax as fresh air was taken in and then released.

"Are you ready?" she asked.

"I think so."

"Okay. Good." She drew in a deep, quiet breath and then slowly let it out. "Imagine a man with long, wavy, chestnut-brown hair. It's all one length and hangs just below his chin. He keeps it tucked behind both ears, but one wayward strand falls stubbornly over his right eye." She paused for a moment.

"I've got it," I said, peaking at her with one eye.

She gave me the thumbs-up sign, and I shut both eyes again.

"Now look at his eyes. They are deep set and as blue as the deepest part of the sea. They twinkle like the brightest stars in the heavens and seem to dance in the moonlight. These are eyes that see only the good in all living things. They are happy, tender, mesmerizing eyes that light up the world around him."

My heart began to melt as I felt the love that he saw through his eyes and imagined he was looking at me.

"His nose is long and narrow with a little round tip on the end. There is nothing particularly unique about this nose except that it has a way of flaring without the slightest provocation, as if it had a mind of its own."

This turned out to be the first of many revelations my mother would have about my father, and I heard her delight in discovering it.

"And then we have his mouth." She chuckled. "How can I possibly describe his mouth?"

I opened my eyes to catch a glimpse of my mother's face, which seemed years younger than I'd ever seen it. It was as though she had traveled back in time for a closer look at the man who had yet to be the father of her only child.

"Ah, ah, ah!" she said, catching me, and then signalled with her finger to shut my eyes. "We don't want to lose what you already have," she cautioned.

I closed my eyes once again as she searched thoughtfully for the right words and then spoke them ever so slowly.

"His mouth was inexplicably tied to whatever was going on behind his eyes." Silence. "This often resulted in a sly, playful smile that curled up just one side of his mouth. It gave you the impression that he had a valuable secret held captive just behind his grin or that his lips were withholding the punch line to the world's greatest joke."

I couldn't keep my eyes shut any longer as I was certain there was more than words written on my mother's face. I was right. She seemed lost in the memory of his mouth as she smiled and slowly shook her head.

"And you could linger there forever," she finally said, "waiting for the one-sided smile to open wide and fill up his face with dimples and ripples of pure, unadulterated joy that poured in and spilled out through those wonderful blue eyes."

I gazed lovingly at my mother as I lay in rapt attention, hanging on to her every word. Her knees were pulled close to her chest, and she hugged her legs, her eyes closed, as she gently rocked his image quietly in her arms.

"That was one of the best things about him," she said, "how everything in him poured out of his eyes. He couldn't help it. Nearly everything made him cry."

I felt the sting of my tears as a smile took hold of my face. She stretched her legs out again and tickled my feet with her toes as she slipped down with her elbows on the arms of her chair, her hands folded across her chest.

"It was delightful to watch for the first time or the hundredth time—the way the laughter would start as little convulsions in his belly. Ha!" she exclaimed, with a puzzled look. "I don't think he ever made a sound." She gazed curiously into the air for affirmation. "Nope." She shook her head. "I can't remember his laughter ever making any noise. It was more like a volcanic eruption that shook his body as it moved upward and then out of the very last place it could be released, which was, of course, his eyes."

She laughed out loud at this thought. "Lava laughs," she dubbed them. We sat together in silence until she shook off the moment. "Now, where was I?"

"You painted his face," I offered.

"Oh yes, I painted his face. How do you like it?"

"It's a wonderful face! I can't believe he had long hair."

"He did. It was perfectly acceptable back then, but that wouldn't have mattered to your father. I'm sure he liked it that way, but I think the real reason he wore it long was because he didn't want to stop whatever he was doing to have it cut. Sitting in a barber's chair for an hour when he could have been outside doing anything else would have been agonizing for him." She chuckled as she began to drift off again.

"I'm glad he had long hair," I said, not knowing what else to say. "Tell me more about how he looked."

"Well, he was not particularly tall, although he was taller than me."

"That wouldn't be hard to do," I chided my mother, who stood just under five feet two.

"True enough." She laughed. "I think Daddy was just about five feet, eleven inches, so he was about a head and a half taller than me. The top of my head didn't quite reach his shoulders."

I tried to picture my mother and father together, which was a challenge. But I didn't want to get hung up at this point, so I said, "Got it," to keep her moving on.

"He was in very good shape. He was an avid swimmer and very active. He loved horseback riding, which he did nearly every day. His body was strong and athletic but lean... not beefy."

The word "beefy" made me laugh.

"And he looked very good in clothes," she said, smiling to herself once again, "which is quite funny, as he cared very little about them. But there was something about the way he dressed that caught your eye. It wasn't the clothes he wore so much as how he wore them. It's hard to explain, and it's kind of a phenomenon now that I think about it. But it was almost as though his clothes came alive with every move he made, yet he was completely unaware of their attachment to him."

I was carefully constructing an image of him in my mind when she said, "But I want to say something that's not about how your father looked, because even though most people considered him attractive, he wasn't what one would think of as a handsome man."

I was disappointed at this statement, mostly because I had just made him very handsome in my mind and hoped I wasn't going to have to start over. She went on with an indisputable truth.

"There was nothing about his appearance that was particularly striking or out of the ordinary by itself. And if you saw him in a room with other men, you might not even notice him. But when he spoke, when he engaged himself with you, he made you feel like you were the most important person in the world. And it wasn't just with me. He was that way with everyone he met. His attention was always on others and never on himself. He could connect with anyone whether they were rich or poor, young or old, happy or sad. He was compassionate and immeasurably kind, and he had a way of comforting those in need and giving hope to those who had none. He was created to encourage and enable others to rise above their circumstances and become more than they dreamed they could be. He was a brilliant light in a dark world. That's what attracted people to him."

"I love that about him!" My heart was about to burst when the "handsome" man came back clearly once again.

"You have all his goodness in you, you know," she said.

I was far more embarrassed by her statement than complimented. I wanted to be a good, kind, compassionate, and selfless person like my father, but I knew I fell far short of those qualities. I saw my role in life as always pleasing others, obeying the rules, and, of course, never being a disappointment to anyone. I thought that if I was the perfect child in everyone's eyes, I could somehow maintain a status quo to life that would ensure nothing bad would ever happen. I considered this my duty, even if it wasn't something I wanted to do. This was what separated me from my dad. His heart was always willing to sacrifice for others, while mine seemed to have no reason for beating. I envied how naturally the sacrifice came to him; but careful not to desire what belonged to someone else, I stopped myself before wanting what he had. "After all," I reminded myself, "no one likes a jealous person."

These thoughts and longings lived inside of me every day, but I never shared them with my mother. I was afraid she might think I was ungrateful for all the things I'd been given or worry about my self-esteem. I never wanted to intentionally upset her, nor did I want to appear less than perfect in her eyes, so I kept these feelings and many others to myself. With her words about my goodness being like my father's hanging in the air, I mustered up a humble smile, thanked her for her kind words, and kept my secrets safe with a simple, "I hope so."

My mouth suddenly gave way to an involuntary yawn, and although my mother must have been glad that I was showing signs of being tired, she was cautious not to end the night before I was ready for sleep.

"So how are you feeling, Miss Lily Johnson, now that you're twelve years old?" she asked, likely being careful not to remind me of how I was feeling when I first climbed into bed.

"Tired," I exclaimed, with no recollection of anything unpleasant having transpired.

"Well, that's not surprising, considering the day that you've had. Birthdays can be quite exhausting, you know."

I smiled with my eyes half-closed as she rose from the comfort of her chair to give me a hug and a kiss on my forehead.

"Sleep tight, my precious Lily. I love you more than the whole wide world."

"I love you too, Mommy," I said without opening my eyes. "This was the best birthday ever."

CHAPTER 6

FAITH, HOPE,
AND LOVE YOU STEW

My birthday weekend was over, and it was time for me to go back to school. I hemmed and hawed that morning, not wanting to leave Spirit for a single moment, let alone an entire day.

"I have an idea," my mother said, trying to get me to move faster than a snail's pace. "Why don't we try out Spirit's new leash? Grab your backpack and lunch bag, and I'll get Spirit. But we must get moving. It'll take longer to get there with the little steps he takes, and we're running a bit late as it is."

It hardly seemed like a suitable alternative to my idea, which was to stay home and play with Spirit all day. But the thought of showing him off to my friends was sufficient motivation to get me moving. And just in time, as the bus arrived at the stop at the same time we did, and the driver opened the doors. Everyone on the bus was peering out the windows to get a better look at Spirit.

"We'll be here when you get home," my mother told me.

I heard a collective "Aww!" from inside the bus.

"That's a very cute puppy, Lily," the driver said. "Is he yours?"

I turned around and blew a kiss to Spirit. "Yes, Mr. Little," I said. "He was my birthday wish. His name is Spirit. Good-bye, Spirit," I called out as the driver shut the doors. Mother held Spirit up and waved one of his paws in a good-bye as the bus slowly pulled away.

Everyone asked about my dog and said things like, "He's adorable!" and "I want one!" I was too proud to be sad. But I couldn't wait to get home.

The first day away from Spirit seemed to take forever, and I was the first one out of the classroom when the final bell rang. Everyone except my friend Maddie had forgotten about the puppy that waved good-bye that morning. Maddie sat next to me on the bus and usually had the seat by the window. But on this day, she offered to give me her seat, so I could see Spirit as soon as we arrived at my stop.

"I hope your mom remembers to bring him," she said.

"She will," I assured her. "She never breaks her promises."

My face was pressed against the window as the bus slowed around the curve that led to my stop, and I stood up a bit prematurely.

"Lily Johnson!' the driver bellowed. "Sit down! That puppy will wait for you."

"Yes, Mr. Little."

I sat back down just before the bus heaved slightly forward and then backward again before coming to a stop. I climbed over Maddie's lap, said good-bye, and hurried toward the open doors.

"Take your time, Miss Lily! He's not going anywhere!" Mr. Little laughed as I jumped from the last step and ran to my mother and Spirit, who wagged his tail and jumped up to kiss me.

"Someone's happy to see you." Mom handed me the leash and took my backpack.

Spirit jumped around and ran between my legs, entangling my feet in his leash. He grabbed hold of it with his teeth and growled as he tugged at it. I was a little bit startled, but Mom just laughed.

"Oh, my heavens!" she said. "He wants to play with you. Give the leash a little tug when he pulls on it but be gentle. You don't want to pull out any of those puppy teeth."

We both laughed as Spirit planted his hind legs firmly on the ground and tried with all his might to get the leash away from me. When he'd had enough tugging, he dropped the lead and pranced proudly down the road toward our house.

This was the time I looked forward to each day...the brief period that existed between arriving home from school and starting homework. Mother recognized my need for downtime when I was in the second grade. That's when homework assignments started, and I had my first meltdown. We used to spend this time taking walks through the woods or just hanging out. But now it was devoted to Spirit. I couldn't wait until the end of the school year, so I could spend more time with him, and I often found myself daydreaming during class about what it would be like to go on adventures with Spirit. Mom and I still didn't know much about otterhounds except that they were hunters and liked to run. Lindenwood had more than enough space for him to run, but the idea of him leaving the property terrified me. On the other hand, I didn't want to keep him on a leash all the time either. I decided to train him as soon as possible.

"He must learn important commands," I reasoned with my mother that night before bedtime. "It will be much safer that way."

"I agree." She winked and gave me a smile. "And a lot more fun!"

"Right. That's what I meant. Anyway, I think I'll start tomorrow."

"That's a wonderful idea, kiddo. The sooner, the better. If you pick up a book from the library, you can start working with him this weekend. I think Spirit is going to do whatever is needed just to be with you, but training him early is a very good idea. It's going to take a lot of patience and effort on your part, you know."

I nodded my head. "And dog treats!" I added. "I'll need dog treats for his rewards. Can you get some?"

"It's a deal." She shook my hand. "You get the book…I'll get the treats."

An image of a fully trained Spirit danced in my head, and my restless feet wiggled beneath the covers as I pictured the two of us running through the open field. Mother sighed as she tried to tuck me in.

"Getting these covers around you is like trying to dress a greased pig," she exclaimed.

I laughed at the thought of my mother trying to put clothes on a well-oiled hog.

"Would you like to hear more of Mira's story? It's been a while since we've visited her."

"Oh yes," I said with a grin, although my mind was still on Spirit.

"Great!" she said. "Let's see. Where did we leave off?"

"Oh, I know," I offered happily. "I remember everything about Mira. She was very happy and beautiful, and she loved everyone, and everyone loved her. But she was too little to worry about not having a reflection, and when her mother and grandmother figured out that she couldn't use mirrors, they decided to keep it a secret from her until she was older."

"Well, that's mostly right." She smiled. "But they didn't tell her about her reflection because they wanted to be certain she fully understood and was comfortable with her inner beauty."

"Oh yeah, I forgot that. What is inner beauty?"

"I'm glad you asked," she said happily. "Inner beauty is something that can only come from your heart. It can't be measured by any physical standard of beauty because it has nothing to do with how we look, but it has everything to do with how we feel and how we make others feel. It is the most perfect kind of beauty there is, and you can't get it from a cream, a blush, or a lipstick. In fact, it has absolutely nothing to do with beautiful hair, a perfect body, or even designer clothes. It shines from within, and those who truly possess it are quite rare indeed, as they have been blessed with everything that truly matters: love, joy, peace, kindness, goodness, patience, and faithfulness."

"That's what Mira had," I remembered.

"Absolutely! But this kind of beauty can't be seen in a mirror. It can only be felt. It's quite a treasure."

"That's what I want someday," I said, wondering what it would be like to feel beautiful.

"You have it now," she said, smiling. Then she continued the story of Mira, a child who was blessed with everything that truly mattered.

"'Mira,' her mother called. 'Dinner!'

"Mira's mother had a lovely voice that sounded like a ringing bell. When she called out for Mira from the porch of their happy home, her words rode on the back of two beautiful lilting notes...one high, one low.

"'Meeer-ahhh! Diii-nahhh!'"

My mother's lovely voice sang the words so sweetly.

"Mira put down her little shovel, brushed the dirt from her tiny hands, and skipped toward the house, singing the notes back to her mother, ''Kaaay, Mahhhm.' Mira loved being outside on almost any kind of day, even when it was cold.

"'That child would live outdoors if you let her,' Grammy would say. 'She's like a snowflake in the winter and a dew-drop in the spring. She belongs out there with the flowers and the trees.'

"'And the birds,' her mother added.

"'Oh yes,' Grammy agreed. 'The birds, the deer, the rabbits. Anything that hops, flies, or runs.'

"They both laughed for a moment, and then they smiled for a very long time.

"'I can't imagine her any other way, Mummy,' said Mira's mother to her darling mum.

"'Neither can I, dear. Neither can I.'

"And the mothers went about the business of seasoning, stirring, lifting, and serving as all mothers do.

"Mira's cheeks were flushed when she walked through the door into the warm kitchen. It was autumn, and the air was cool and crisp (something that went unnoticed until she stepped into the cozy room). Mira had been playing in the field by the little stream all day, building a small house of twigs, mud, and grass for the rabbits to nestle in during the winter. She did this every year, and although she never actually saw bunnies living there, she didn't want to disappoint any would-be inhabitants who might be secretly depending upon her for shelter from the cold.

"'Winters in U-R-Here can be quite difficult if you're a creature without a home,' she once declared. 'I think I shall make them a small place to live that keeps the weather outside where it belongs.' And so, she did. Stepping inside her not-too-big-not-too-small dwelling, she noticed that the house felt particularly wonderful and smelled almost heavenly. And she said so.

"'What are you making, Grammy? It smells heavenly.'

"Her grandmother stood over a large pot of stew that was well stocked with vegetables, beef, and barley. This was Mira's favorite dish when the weather was crisp and her stomach quite empty.

"'Love You Stew and pumpkin bread,' Grammy said. Then she chuckled. 'But it's not for little girls covered in mud.'

"Mira looked down at her clothes, which were caked with dirt. 'Oops,' she said. Then she did a quick about-face back to the porch where she removed her shoes, brushed off her clothes and wiped the excess earth from her hands before making another entrance.

"'I'll go wash up, Gram. The food smells so good. Thank you! Thank you! Thank you!'

"It is my pleasure, little one,' Grammy called out.

"Mira ran down the hall and up the stairs to get ready for a big bowl of Grammy's Love You Stew and pumpkin bread.

"Mira's bedroom was on the second floor of her not-too-big-not-too-small house, and it was just one door down from Grammy's room. The room where her parents slept was across the hall from Mira and Grammy, as was the main bath. Grammy had a small bathroom, but Mira shared with her parents.

"The main bath was a bright white room with a blue and white tiled floor, a gleaming white pedestal sink, and a great big white tub with four clawed feet. One large window overlooked the side yard. Mira's Grammy had made beautiful light-blue gossamer curtains for it that had tiny white flowers along the edge, which she had embroidered herself. A single closet was located on the wall that was opposite the sink, where her mother kept the soap, shampoo, and all the fresh, clean linens and towels. Mira thought they smelled like summer, and she loved to bury her face in a newly laundered towel before drying off after a bath.

"There was also a medicine cabinet just above the sink that Mira was not allowed to open. Being a very good and obedient little girl, she never did. She often wondered what was behind the small door as she stood on the stool in front of the sink. But she dismissed her thoughts, as doing otherwise would only lead to trouble. Trouble was something Mira never cared to know.

"'Why ask for trouble when you can ask for so many wonderful things instead?' Grammy once said.

"From that day on, Mira only asked for things that made people happy and pleased the One Who Provides.

"By the time Mira had taken a bath, washed her face and hands, brushed her hair, and changed her clothes, there was more than just stew brewing in the kitchen. She quickly ran down the steps toward the voices and laughter to join the group of people who were now milling about. Some folks were placing dishes and flatware on the table; others were cutting bread or pouring lemonade. Mira's mother was smiling ear-to-ear as she and Grammy miraculously pulled more delicious-smelling food out of what seemed to be thin air. But when Mira entered the room, everyone stopped what they were doing and turned their attention to her.

"'Mira! How are you today?'

"'Mira! So happy to see you!'

"'Mira! Bunny huts again this year? Bravo!'

"'Mira! Mira! Mira!'

"There were kisses and hugs and pinching of cheeks as Mira giggled her way to a pile of neatly folded napkins, which she placed next to each plate. Soon the food was prepared and found its way to the center of the table. There were large crocks and ladles for the stew, baskets of bread, butter, and an array of vegetables that were fresh from the garden.

"'How do you make such a wonderful stew, Grammy?' Mr. Wallace asked. He was a frequent visitor to Mira's home, and while he was fond of the stew, he was even fonder of Grammy.

"'Oh, Mr. Wallace, I don't do anything special.' Grammy blushed. 'There's just a lot of love in Love You Stew.'

"Mira noticed the twinkle in Mr. Wallace's eyes as he looked at Grammy, and that made her smile.

"'Well, your stew is a blessing to me,' Mr. Wallace said. He raised his glass in a toast. 'As are all of you.'

"Everyone at the table clinked their glasses and nodded as Mira's father said, 'Let us bow our heads and give thanks to the One Who Provides for the blessing of family, friends, and food for our bodies as well as our souls.'

"'Amen!' they all said.

"Someone added, 'And for Love You Stew!'

"Everyone said, 'Amen!'

"The talking and laughter continued until the last bite was bitten and the last sip was supped. After dinner some people stayed to help with the dishes; some stayed just to be there awhile longer. Mira took what little scraps were left outside and placed them by the big tree in the backyard for her woodland friends. Then she went back in the house to find her father's lap, where she curled up tight and fell fast asleep.

"The sun peeked through her window the next morning and beckoned her to rise and shine. Little Mira sat up in her lovely pink bed, and after a single stretch and a quick yawn, she threw back the covers and jumped to the floor, ready to welcome the day. Mira remembered the food she had left under the big tree and climbed up on her window seat to look outside. She had to lean in on the deep sill and get very close to the glass to see the big tree. But sure enough, the food was gone!

"Mira wished she had seen who, or what, had eaten it. She imagined it was a beautiful fawn with her mother, and she said loud enough for them to hear, 'You're very welcome, of course! I'm glad that you enjoyed it. And I hope you'll come again.' Then she climbed down from the seat beneath the window and skipped off to see who else was awake.

"Mira heard her grandmother singing in the kitchen, and a wisp of baked apples and cinnamon touched her nose as she hurried down the hall. She knew something wonderful was baking for breakfast.

"'Grammy! Grammy!' she cried out from the hall. 'The food is gone from under the tree! Someone had a feast last night.'

"'Oh, gracious me! That is very exciting news. Do you know who our guests were?'

"'No. But I imagine it was the new fawn I saw by the woods with her mother.'

"'Well,' said Grammy, 'you should go outside and take a look. Perhaps you'll find some hoofprints by the tree.'

"Mira grabbed her jacket from the hall closet, slipped on her rubber boots, and ran to the yard to search for clues.

"The morning was still very young, and the sun had not yet dried the dew from the earth. This made Mira's job quite easy, as the footprints from the hungry visitors were still imprinted in the blanket of wet grass that covered the ground. Just as she had suspected, two sets of hooves—one big, one small—led from the wooded area nearby directly to the tree.

"'It *was* the deer!' she exclaimed happily. Then she noticed that tiny paw prints were around the feeding place as well. 'And the rabbits! Oh, how delightful! They must have had a dinner party too.' She ran back to the house to share the news with Grammy, who had just taken fresh-baked apple cobbler out of the oven.

"Mira's father walked into the kitchen, rubbing his belly. 'Mmm! Something smells good enough to eat,' he said, smiling.

"'It's Grammy's cobbler, Daddy. It smells so delicious.'

"Her father hugged his daughter playfully while pretending to take a bite of her hand. 'Not as delicious as you!' he chortled.

"Mira giggled and scrunched herself into his loving arms as he said, 'Good morning, my precious one. And a very good morning to you, my dearest Petra.'

"He took an exaggerated whiff of the cobbler that Grammy was taking from the oven and said, 'Heavenly! You are truly a blessing on this glorious day.'

"'Blessings to you, son-in-law,' Grammy said with a smile. 'You are right on time this morning.'

"Mira's mother appeared at the basement door with an armful of newly laundered towels. 'Good morning, family,' she said. 'Save me a seat; I'll be right back.'

"'We won't begin without you,' Grammy assured her as she placed the hearty warm cobbler on the table next to a pitcher of cream.

"Mira's mother soon reappeared and sat down in the chair next to her only child. Then everyone joined hands and bowed their heads as they gave thanks to the One Who Provides.

"After the amen, Mira's father eyed the cobbler and with a big smile said, 'Mmm! I believe that big one in the middle has my name on it.'

"The steaming cobbler was still quite warm, so Mira's mother poured a bit of cold cream on top of Mira's portion, which cooled it down just enough to take a bite.

"'Oh Grammy, this is the best cobbler ever!'

"'Dear me!' Grammy chuckled. 'I do believe you say that about *every* cobbler!'

"'Why, of course,' said Mira's mother. 'That's because the best is always what we have right now.' And everyone agreed.

"After his plate was nearly clean, Mira's father said, 'This is the way we start our day. How very blessed we are.' He bowed his head for a moment and then looked at his family and smiled. 'What does everyone have planned for the day?' he asked as he carried his empty plate to the kitchen sink.

"'Well,' chimed in Mother, 'today we will work on math and history.'

"'Yay!' shouted Mira. 'I love history.'

"'Not too fond of math, though,' said her father with a wink.

"Her mother smiled. 'No, not too fond of math. But she's doing fine. Perhaps we'll start with math and be done with it. Then we'll take a little break and finish school on a positive historical note.'

"Mira smiled and nodded. 'What are you doing today, Grammy?' she asked.

"'Oh, I have a few chores I need to take care of, and then I'm going to visit Sarah Martin. Poor dear. She fell the other day and isn't getting around as well as she should. Some women from the church are taking turns helping her until she's back on her feet. I thought I might bring along the quilt I've been working on to give us something to do together. I believe Sarah loves quilting. I baked an extra cobbler for her. I know she loves cobbler.'

"'Not as much as I do,' said Father as he grinned and patted his belly once again. 'Well, ladies,' he added, 'thank you for your wonderful company and for a truly delicious breakfast. I love you all! But now I suspect it's time for me to be on my way.' And with that, he kissed each of his three girls on the tops of their heads and gave Mira a hug as he whistled a happy tune and walked out the door.

"'Mira,' said her mother when breakfast was over, 'I'll help Grammy with the dishes. Why don't you take the cobbler crusts out to the yard? I think the birds might like some yummy crumbs.'

"'Oh yes. There were deer and rabbits here last night, but we mustn't forget the birds.'

"After Mira was out the door, her mother said to Grammy, 'Mum, Mira is growing into a lovely, kind, generous girl, don't you think?'

"'Why, of course, darling! She is filled with the light of the Spirit.'

"'I know,' her mother said, gazing out the window at her only child. 'But we can't protect her from the world forever. How will we know when it's time to tell her the truth?'

"Grammy looked at her daughter through eyes of great compassion and wisdom. 'He will let you know when it's time, dear. Protecting her is His job, not ours.'

"The two watched as Mira carefully spread the crusts evenly under the elm tree and then danced after a butterfly that flitted from flower to flower.

"'She's like a beacon,' Mira's mother said, mesmerized by her child's every move.

"'She certainly is,' Grammy agreed. 'Shining for others who need to find their way. She will understand this one day, and when she does, it will serve her life's purpose. Until then, be strong and of good cheer. It is all part of His great plan. We are never, ever alone.'

"Mira's mother hugged her lovely mum, and together they said thank you to the One Who Provides and praised His goodness. And the Spirit was with them."

Mother closed the pages of her imaginary book, signaling that the reading was over for the night.

"Is the Spirit that's with them their dog?" I asked groggily. My ability to grasp what my mother would answer was fading quickly, as sleep was bearing down on me.

"No, dear. But I think you'll be surprised at what the two Spirits have in common."

"Mommy," I said with heavy eyes, "is God the One Who Provides?"

She sighed and then smiled. "Yes, honey. The One is God."

"Then why don't they just call him God?"

Mother laughed as if she'd been caught off guard, and then she said thoughtfully, "Well...if you think about it... God is the Provider. I mean...He created all things, so He provides life. And the living things He has given us can be used for food, clothing, and shelter. So He provides for all our needs." She was still for a moment while her eyes searched the room. "Yes," she concluded, "it seems like an appropriate name for Him."

I still had a lot of questions, but the answer she gave made sense, so I decided to let it go for the time being. I was having a very hard time staying awake, and there was something I needed to know before giving in to sleep. I rolled over and propped my head up with one hand as I looked deep into her eyes.

"Do you believe in God?" I asked.

My mother didn't respond quickly, although I believed she knew the answer. The very little she had told me about her parents always included their love for God. She once said that Christ was at the center of everything they did, said, and touched because they wanted to be like Him. So they put the needs of others before their own and prayed in thanks for the little they had every day. When they died my mother must have prayed that God would send someone to save her from the orphanage. But only Myrtle came. Looking back, I think my question gave her pause when she realized she hadn't stopped believing in a loving God. She'd just stopped believing He loved her.

"Yes, Lily. I believe in God."

"Then why don't we pray?"

"I've been thinking about that myself lately." She sounded sincere but tenuous. "It's something we should do. My father used to say that we should thank God for all things, big and small. I'm afraid I haven't done that in a very long time. And," she said with a loving smile, "I have a lot to be thankful for."

I waited for a moment, expecting to hear a prayer. But there was only reverent silence.

"So, is that it?" I asked. "Silence? Is that all there is to prayer?" I was disappointed but at the same time happy that it was so simple.

My mother laughed nervously. It had clearly been many years since she'd bowed before the Father.

"Well, I think it can be," she said hopefully. "I do remember one prayer my parents taught me when I was a little girl. It goes like this:

"Now I lay me down to sleep,

"I pray the Lord my soul to keep.

"If I should die before I wake,

"I pray the Lord my soul to take.

"Oh my!" she said with a horrified look. "I don't recall it being so terrifying. I'm pretty sure we can come up with something better than that." She chuckled. "I'll give it some thought, and we can try again tomorrow."

"Okay," I agreed. "I'll give it some thought too."

But I let the thought go as my tired eyes began to close, and I soon found myself dreaming of apple cobbler, bunny huts, and running through an open field with my bold otterhound. She leaned down and kissed my cheek after turning out the light and said a brief but very important prayer.

"Thank you, Father, for my precious Lily."

CHAPTER 7

THE DAY THINGS WENT HORRIBLY WRONG

My thoughts were fully focused on finding the right dog-training book as my mother handed me my lunch bag, and we headed out the door for the bus.

"You probably won't find anything specific on otter-hounds," my mother offered before saying good-bye for the day. "But I'm sure there will be something on basic training in the library."

"Thanks, Mom. I hope so." I walked onto the bus and shared my dog-training plans with Maddie.

"Finch will have something," she said, eager to help.

"Yeah," I agreed. "And she'll know right where it is."

Maddie laughed. "I know! She's like a robot or something. She knows where every single book is and its stupid number."

"I know!" I said, nodding my head. "Who memorizes stuff like that?"

"She kind of freaks me out," Maddie snarled.

"Ha-ha! You can say that again."

The morning dragged as I waited anxiously for lunch. I decided to eat as quickly as possible and take the extra time before class to go to the library. Summer break would be here before I knew it, and I wanted to have plenty of time to read the book before school let out. Miss Finch, the librarian, was a real stickler about returning books on time, and I knew she'd be particularly anxious with the end of the year so close. Ordinarily, I would have searched for the book on my own rather than bother her. But having limited time before lunch break would be over, I decided to ask Miss Finch for help.

Standing stoically behind the circular counter that served as an office, computer station, and information center, Miss Finch was too deeply engrossed in whatever task was at hand to notice me. A short, thin, plain-looking woman with perfect posture and angular features, she had a habit of peering at you over a pair of reading glasses that were perpetually perched upon the bridge of her pointy nose. She considered library science to be among the greatest advancements in history and viewed her occupation to be on par with that of a great surgeon, scientist, or world leader. She was very proud of her occupation and took it, as well as herself, quite seriously. Too seriously, if you asked me! In all the years I had been going to the school library, I never once saw her smile. Nor had I ever heard her call anyone by their name. She chose instead to glare at people from over the top of her frames as though you had just interrupted her. It was very disconcerting and seemed unnecessarily rude, to me.

"Perhaps she is memorizing the Dewey Decimal System," my mother joked after one of my full-on rants about Miss Finch's lack of personality.

"I don't think she's even human," I protested. "She never says hello or thank-you or even you're welcome! It's like she's from another planet."

"Well," my mother said, chuckling, "not everyone can be bubbling over with personality, you know. It takes all kinds to make the world."

But Miss Finch's kind was one that I would rather do without as I stood under the sign that gave the promise of "Information," trying to get her attention. After clearing my throat for what felt like the hundredth time, she shifted her gaze up and over her eyeglasses without ever moving her head.

"May I help you?" she whispered indignantly.

"Yes, please," I said quietly. "I'm looking for a book on dog training."

"Dog training would be classified under 636.70835, in aisle ten. Is this a school project?"

I hesitated before answering, fearing she might put a halt to my quest for knowledge if it wasn't a requirement. "No, ma'am. It's personal."

My comment caused her to stand even more erect as she tilted her head backward and looked at me through thick glass with an owl-like gaze.

"You realize that school ends for the summer in exactly nine and one-half days? School days, that is. Not personal days." She drew her eyebrows upward until they nearly reached her hairline. "Books that are borrowed from the library for any reason must be returned within ten school days. But because the school year will be ending in nine and one-half days, any book you borrow today must be returned two and one-half days prior to the end of the school year, which means it must be in the library by the end of the school day on the twelfth day of June. Do not presume that because you are borrowing a book for personal reasons that the rules do not apply. If it is not returned by the end of the school on the twelfth day of June, you can expect a fine of thirty-six cents per day per book to be applied until the book or books are returned. You're aware of that rule, are you not?"

"Yes, ma'am. I'm aware of the rule," I lied.

"And should you fail to return the book before the school year ends, the fine will continue through the summer and will include not just weekdays but weekends as well. At thirty-six cents per day, the fine would be quite significant. Do you know how much this one book will cost you for your personal use if it is not returned on time?"

I hadn't done the math, but her warning was more than enough to convince me that being late in returning the book was not something I wanted to do. "Yes, ma'am. It's a lot," I said. "I'll make sure I have the book back on time." I scurried off to the safety of aisle ten.

The books in aisle ten were categorized by author, so it took a while to find the only book in the entire library on dog training. "Yes!" I hissed when I spotted it and quickly glanced through the chapter titled "Basic Commands." "That'll do," I said and hurried back to the front desk to check out.

Miss Finch was still absorbed in her manual and did not acknowledge my presence.

"Excuse me," I said. I was beginning to worry about making it to class before the bell rang.

Miss Finch lifted her eyes above her rims. "May I help... oh, it's you. Did you find what you were looking for?"

"Yes, ma'am. It's a book on dog training."

Miss Finch took the book. "So, it is." She punched some numbers into her computer and pointed out the return date indicated on my receipt. "There is a financial penalty if you are late," she reminded me.

"Yes, ma'am. Thirty-six cents a day. I won't be late." I ran out the door just as the bell rang for class to begin.

I tried to sneak into my classroom quietly, and I would have been successful if I hadn't tripped over Billy Gaberchevski's backpack on the way to my seat and slam my knee against the side of his chair. Even that wouldn't have been so bad if Billy hadn't yelled, "Hey! Watch where you're going, moron!" and everyone in the class, including the teacher, turned to see me limp back toward my desk.

"You're late, Miss Johnson." Mr. Wicket put the chalk on the blackboard ledge and glared at me.

"Yes, sir. I'm sorry. I was in the library."

"You were in the library? You were supposed to be at lunch!"

"Well, I was at lunch, sir, but I wanted to get a book, so I left lunch early and went to the library."

"And who gave you permission to leave the lunchroom early? Did someone give you a hall pass?" His response, as well as his tone, was completely unexpected, and I sensed I had done something terribly wrong.

"No, Mr. Wicket," I answered nervously. "I didn't have a hall pass."

His eyes bulged, and his lips pursed as he sat down at his desk and began scribbling something on a piece of paper.

"Well, then, Miss Johnson, I will be happy to give you one now. This one," he said, writing furiously, "will take you to the principal's office, where you will explain to him your reason for being late as well as why you were wandering in the halls without permission."

"The principal's office? Oh Mr. Wicket! No! Please, sir! I wasn't really wandering. I went directly from the lunchroom to the library and then here. And I was only late by a minute. It won't happen again, Mr. Wicket. I promise!"

But the note had already been written, and his decision was irrevocable. He held on to the piece of paper and thrust his hand toward me with his arm extended like a sword.

"It's a little late for apologies, Miss Johnson," he said, without moving a muscle. "Come up here now and take this to Mr. Rubello. He will be the one to decide how to deal with this matter."

I couldn't believe what was happening. I got up from my seat and walked toward the front of the class as everyone began talking in hushed tones and giggles.

"And take your backpack with you," he said as I turned and walked toward the door. "You might not be coming back to the classroom today."

I looked back at him with a sorrowful gaze. Not coming back? My head was spinning as I walked forlornly through the empty hall toward the principal's office. I thought I might throw up. I'd never done anything wrong before, and I couldn't imagine why Mr. Wicket was being so mean. I was a very good student, after all, with a perfect attendance record. Shouldn't that count for something?

Mrs. Olson, the school secretary, greeted me as I walked through the door of the administration office. "Why, hello, Lily!" she said cheerfully as an overpowering scent of lilac perfume wafted through the air. "And to what do we owe this pleasure?"

"It's not a pleasure, Mrs. Olson," I said, handing her the hall pass with the note from my teacher.

"Oh my!" She read the note without looking up. "This is serious stuff." She chuckled until she realized I was about to cry. "Oh dear! No, no, no! Don't cry, Lily. I'm so sorry. I was only teasing you," she said apologetically. "You have absolutely nothing to worry about, Lily, and I'm sure Mr. Rubello will agree with me. Why, I don't know of anyone with a more spotless record than you. You are a model student," she said, handing me a box of tissues. "This is undoubtedly a great big misunderstanding. I'm sure of it."

I smiled as I wiped away my tears and blew my nose. I was so grateful for her kindness and was beginning to feel a little better.

"Thank you, Mrs. Olson. I hope you're right."

"Yes, yes, of course I am, dear. I'm going to go speak to Mr. Rubello right now and explain things to him." She gave me a reassuring smile as she trotted off toward the principal's office with the cursed note in her hand.

It felt like an hour had passed before she reappeared with a sheepish look on her face, as though she were the one in trouble. I looked up hopefully.

"Mr. Rubello will see you now, Lily." As I walked past her desk, she whispered half-heartedly, "Don't be afraid, dear."

But I was afraid. Mr. Rubello was like a drill sergeant. He was a short man with a military build, who looked as though he was perpetually standing at attention in his over-starched white shirts and navy-blue ties. He never spoke to anyone without giving them orders, and even when he welcomed the students at our assemblies, his words came with an unspoken warning to "Sit up straight, and do not fidget." I made a mental note about my posture before entering the room.

Mr. Rubello's slicked-back black hair peeked over the back of his big leather chair, where he sat facing the window. He didn't bother to swivel toward me when I walked through the door of his office. Did he even know that I was there?

"You may take a seat, Miss Johnson," he said, speaking to the window.

My heart pounded in my chest as my face flushed. When he finally spun his chair in my direction, it almost seemed like he was expecting someone else. He glanced at a manila folder that he held on his lap and then slapped it down on the desk.

"I am very surprised to see you in my office in this capacity, Miss Johnson." He opened the folder one more time. "Miss *Lily* Johnson," he confirmed. "Yes. Well, I understand from Mrs. Olson that you are one of our better students." He looked through the folder again. "Humph!" He smirked. "And...one of the more privileged, as well."

I had no idea what he meant by that remark, but his words seemed to make him angry. He took a short breath through his nose and quickly blew it from his lips.

"But I suppose that is neither here nor there," he concluded. "The question that is currently on the table is…what you were doing during the lunch hour that made you late to class? Can you answer that question, Miss Johnson?" His tone was not at all reassuring, and he quickly became impatient when I didn't offer an immediate response. "Come, come, Miss Johnson. I don't have all day."

I felt helpless and nearly too terrified to speak.

"What was going through my mind?" I whispered into my lap.

"Speak up, Miss Johnson!" the principal barked. "And lift up your head. How do you expect to defend yourself if I'm unable to hear you?"

"Yes, sir," I said, more loudly than I intended. Then I cleared my throat and began again. "Well, sir, I was just thinking that I wanted to get a book from the library."

"I see," he said, jotting something down in my file. "And what did you do after you had this thought?"

I had to work very hard to recall anything that happened even moments before this one, as my frightened mind had begun to shut down. I cleared my throat again and spoke in his direction.

"I believe I cleaned off my area at the table, threw away my garbage, and then went to the library. I checked the clock before I left, though, and there was a full twenty minutes before the bell rang. I was sure I had plenty of time to get to class."

"So you decided there was something *you* wanted, and having no regard for the rules, you took it upon yourself to simply get what you wanted without asking for permission." Principal Rubello sat back in his big leather chair with his hands folded across his chest and a very pious look on his face.

"Rules are rules, Miss Johnson," he said emphatically. "And they apply to everyone in this school. That includes you."

"But, sir," I said honestly, "I always follow the rules!"

The chair rolled back just far enough for him to take a superior stance as he glared down from his position of authority. "Is that so? Then why didn't you ask one of the lunch ladies to give you a hall pass?"

"I don't know," I stammered. "I guess I didn't think I needed one." My lower lip was quivering uncontrollably as the word "guilty" flashed before my eyes. A flush of red crept up from beneath the principal's starched white collar and flooded his face.

"You didn't think you needed one." He snapped his middle finger with his thumb. It was the loudest snap I'd ever heard, and it echoed through my head as he snapped and paced back and forth, back and forth. I began to tremble as my mind reeled through the events in the lunchroom.

"No, sir. There was a book that I wanted very much to get from the library, and I thought I had enough time to do that before class started. But when I got to the library, Miss Finch was busy and didn't help me right away. When I finally found the book, she was still too busy to check me out. And that's why I was late."

Mr. Rubello stopped dead in his tracks and clasped his hands behind his back.

"Being late is not the primary offense, Miss Johnson," he said as his nostrils flared. "The primary offense is not having a hall pass. Not having a hall pass shows a blatant disregard for the rules of this institution, which simply will not be tolerated!"

"Yes, sir," I said, with my guilty head bowed.

Mr. Rubello tucked his left arm behind his back and glared down at me from behind his desk. He stood perfectly still as he twirled a large-barrelled fountain pen between the fingers of his right hand, and I thought for a moment that I might be crushed by the weight of judgment that filled the room.

"Did Miss Finch ask you for a hall pass?" the principal asked as he held his pose.

"No, sir. But she reminded me about the financial penalty for returning a book late. Twice."

"I see." He wrote Miss Finch's name in bold letters on a pad of paper.

I was now afraid I had just gotten Miss Finch into trouble, which, as it turned out, I had.

"And Mr. Wicket," he said, tapping the tip of his pen on the desk. "Tell me about him. Why do you suppose he felt that it was necessary to send you to my office rather than give you a warning? I'm assuming, of course, that this was the first time you've been caught breaking a rule?"

"Oh yes, sir! I mean…no, sir! I've never broken a rule."

"If that, in fact, is the case, then why would he take such drastic measures? It seems a bit unreasonable to me. Does it seem unreasonable to you, Miss Johnson?"

Everything seemed unreasonable to me at that point.

"I don't know why Mr. Wicket decided to send me to your office," I blurted. "He's never acted irrationally before."

"Mmm…hmm," he muttered. "I don't believe I used the word 'irrational,' but it seems as good a word as any." Then he wrote down Mr. Wicket's name and included "irrational" in all caps next to it.

"Frankly, Miss Johnson," he said, shuffling the papers in my file, "I don't know what to do with you. On the one hand, this is the first reported infraction against you in your history at this school. By every indication it appears that you are an acceptable student with a good attendance record. That, of course, will work in your favor."

He took a few steps and then hooked his thumbs through his belt in a power stance as he concluded, "But I can't let you off the hook entirely, now, can I? What kind of example would that set? What would the parents of this fine community think if I, the principal of this school, were to overlook the rules and allow any student who cared to roam the halls to do so without a pass? For that matter what would our superintendent think?" He paused as he garnered the answers to his questions.

"I'll tell you what he would think, Miss Johnson. He would think I was incapable of doing my job and that I don't have the backbone required to keep a tight reign over the vandals and hooligans who run amuck in this school and in this very town. He would think that the recent behavior of a bunch of scoundrels who have nothing better to do with their time than to spew garbage through our pristine streets was the result of a lack of discipline within these walls and that I am slacking off when it is clearly the time to kick butt and take names. But let me tell you, Miss Johnson, nothing could be further from the truth. You'll see pigs fly before you see those trash bags take me down. You can bet your perfect attendance on that!"

The principal slammed the folder onto the desk and turned, once again, to the safety of the world outside his window as he composed himself and his thoughts.

"In light of today's events," he began, his back facing me, "I believe it is appropriate that you spend the rest of the day here in my office and write one hundred times in this notebook, 'I will obey the rules.'" He pivoted on the heel of one foot and then marched toward his desk and handed me a pencil and notebook. "One hundred times, Miss Johnson," he ordered as he checked his watch. "You may begin…now." He left the room and slammed the door behind him.

I sat stunned for a moment, unable to move. "What just happened?" I asked myself. "Has everyone gone mad?" I looked down at the notebook as my eyes filled with tears and ran down my disgruntled face.

"If Finch had asked me for a hall pass, I wouldn't be in this position right now," I said to the paper. I pounded my fist on the arm of the chair and declared, "Stupid Finch," just under my breath.

I will obey the rules. I will obey the rules.

"And what is up with Wicket and Rubello?"

I will obey the rules. I will obey the rules.

"The two of them have absolutely lost it!"

I will obey the rules. I will obey the rules.

"Maybe they're aliens," I snarled, "and the real Wicket and Rubello are being held captive in an invisible spaceship that's hovering above the town." I shook my head, deciding not to let them off the hook that easily. I looked at the clock. School would be over soon, and this horrible day would go with it. I continued writing and finished the hundredth time when the bell rang for dismissal. I dropped the notebook and pencil on Mr. Rubello's desk. Grateful that I didn't have to go back to my class, I grabbed my backpack and walked quickly out of the principal's office past Mrs. Olson and a cluster of people who were waiting to speak to her.

"Have a good night, Lily," she called out, turning her attention from the group to me. Then she cried out, "Oh dear," as I ran past her without saying a word.

I figured out later that that was another big mistake, since everyone waiting to speak to her would have wanted to know what was wrong with Lily Johnson; and Mrs. Olson, being a woman of great compassion but not much wisdom, would surely have shared the troubling story with them. And, most likely, those who'd just witnessed my rudeness would be quick to judge and even quicker to tell others about their first-hand experience with "the other side of the Johnson girl."

"I would never have believed it if I hadn't seen it with my own eyes," they would say, and the news of my shocking behavior would spread through the town like wildfire.

Being impolite, it seemed, was on par with throwing garbage throughout the town and, as I discovered, would simply not be tolerated. I didn't mean to be impolite. But the building and everything in it had begun to feel toxic, and I couldn't wait to be outside to breathe the fresh air. I saw the sunlight shining through the doors in front of me and could almost taste the sweet smell of freedom when I felt someone grab me by the back of my shirt.

"And just where do you think you're going, Miss Johnson?" It was the principal.

"I'm going home, sir. School is over, and I have to get to my bus."

"Did you finish your assignment?"

"Yes, sir, I did. It's on your desk. Now may I please go home?"

He had nothing else to hold me with, yet he wouldn't let go of my shirt. My lip quivered as his eyes filled with rage; then the anger I had experienced earlier welled up inside me once again. This time it carried the revelation that I was being treated unfairly. I jerked my shoulder away from his grasp and left his empty hand suspended in mid-air. I looked him in the eye, but I didn't say a word.

As I turned and walked quickly toward my bus, he yelled, "Dismissed!"

The altercation with Rubello nearly made me miss my bus, and Mr. Little was about to pull away when I knocked loudly on the door, and the other students yelled for him to stop. I was exhausted from the events of the day, and my legs felt weak as I climbed up the bus steps, and the door closed behind me.

"You're late, Miss Lily," Mr. Little said without a smile.

"No kidding," I thought as I kept my eyes fixed on the open spot next to Maddie. The stagnant bus air was making me sick to my stomach, and I wanted more than anything to be home. I felt like a jackhammer was going off in my head when I dropped down into my seat, too wasted to say hello to Maddie, who was leaning toward me like a mother hen.

I knew she was just concerned, but the hovering was making me claustrophobic. I wished she'd back away, so I could breathe.

"Are you okay, Lil?" she asked with a worried look on her face.

I wanted to tell her I was fine, but I had a sickeningly sour taste in my throat that made my mouth water profusely, and all I could do was swallow repeatedly while I prayed to God that He would not let me throw up. After about the nine hundredth swallow, the horrible taste began to go away, but I was terrified that it might come back. So I sat perfectly still; took in short, shallow breaths of air; and waited for the queasiness to subside.

I knew that the kid who sat across the aisle was staring at me with some degree of intensity, and it made me very uncomfortable. I wanted to look back at him, just to make him stop, but lifting my head triggered a sick sensation in the back of my neck, so I glanced at him from the corner of my eye. It almost seemed like he was in a trance, but at the same time, he appeared to be praying. Or possibly begging. Whatever he was doing, he sure wasn't stopping.

I thought he was being terribly rude at a particularly tough time. Then I remembered one very hot day in the beginning of the year. We were on our way home from school, and he suddenly turned a yucky shade of green. Without a single word of warning, he puked up his lunch and what looked like a whole bag of partially chewed, sugarcoated sour candy that smelled so bad, everyone else on the bus almost puked up their lunches too. Mr. Little stopped the bus and walked toward the boy with a handful of paper towels and a half-empty bottle of water and did his best to clean up the runny chunks that landed mostly on the boy's backpack and the seat in front of him. Unfortunately, there weren't enough paper towels or water to take care of the gooey slime that was on the boy's pants and shoes. He had to ride the rest of the way to his stop smelling like throw up and listening to the creeps in the back of the bus making fun of him. One particularly mean kid stuck his head out the bus window and made vomiting noises at the sick kid, who was walking as fast as he could toward his house.

This might have been the worst thing I could have thought about at that particular time, as the rancid smell of regurgitated candy filled up my brain and curled up my nose. I was certain that I was going to lose it when my stomach miraculously settled down and I knew I would be okay. Turning my head ever so slightly toward the boy, I smiled. But I don't think he noticed. I can understand that. Anyone who's had the misfortune of throwing up on a school bus or anywhere in public knows it's one of the most humiliating things that can ever happen to you. Some kids, like the boy across the aisle from me, never fully recover. Even if you manage to put that fateful day behind you, there will always be creeps like the kids in the back of the bus who are waiting to make fun of you all over again.

My head had stopped pounding, and the bad taste was gone from my mouth, but it wasn't long before my eyes welled up with tears and my nose began to run. I looked to Maddie for help, but before I said a word, she'd already pulled out a pack of tissues and handed them to me with a smile.

"Thanks," I said, after blowing my nose.

"No prob," she assured me. "Everyone gets sick." She glanced over at the boy, who had finally turned away. "So, what's going on? Do you think you're coming down with something?" Maddie was sincerely concerned about me, but I was too wiped out to talk.

"I don't know. Maybe." I lowered my head once again.

Not sharing everything that happened that day with Maddie might not have seemed like a big deal. But it turned out to be very big, as it was just one of many seemingly innocent things that wound up in a mountainous pile of mistakes that I would not soon get over.

We rode the rest of the way in silence, although once in a while she'd turn to me and smile. She smiled at the boy across the aisle from me too, even though he wasn't paying attention.

Things only got worse when we arrived at my stop, as my mother and Spirit weren't there to meet me. I leaned over Maddie and looked up and down the street, but they were nowhere in sight. As soon as the bus came to a full stop, I jumped up from my seat and made a mad dash for the doors.

"Where could they be?" I wondered as I stepped off the bus and watched it slowly pull away.

Everyone was staring at me from the back window, and I felt painfully alone as I walked quickly past the dense trees and wrought iron fence that separated Mrs. Robbins' property from the rest of the world. The feeling intensified when I reached the front gate and found that it was closed.

"It's never closed during the day," I thought.

My heart was pounding as I poked at the keypad that activated the hydraulics and squeezed through the gate before it could fully open. My backpack got stuck on the latch and I yanked it as hard as I could just as the gate released it, which nearly sent me tumbling to the ground. Looking down the alley of giant white elm trees that covered the only path to the house, I saw my mom and Spirit meandering toward me.

"Hey," she waved cheerfully as I ran frantically toward her. "You're early!" she called out.

Every bit of life seemed to rush out of me as my shoulders fell forward and my head dropped back. I felt like an old rag doll whose stuffing had been knocked out of her.

"I thought you were dead!" I cried.

"Oh, honey," she said, suddenly aware that I was in crisis mode. "We're fine!"

Stating the obvious made her laugh, and I lightened up a bit when Spirit grabbed one of my shoestrings and growled as he gave it a tug.

"I'm so, so sorry, Lil," Mom said as we walked toward the cottage. "I guess I lost track of the time. I didn't mean to frighten you."

"Oh, Mommy, this has been the worst day ever!"

She took my face in her hands as she smiled and pulled me toward her. "Well, my darling, you're home now," she said as our foreheads touched. "Let's go in, so you can tell me all about it."

The weight of the world was lifted from me when she put her arm around my shoulder. Spirit ran in front of us and then behind as he entangled us in his dangling leash, and we giggled as we stumbled toward the back door of our cottage, tripping over ourselves, the dog, and each other.

"Spirit, stop!" my mom commanded half-heartedly. He paid no attention. "This dog needs training," she declared. "I hope we can find a good book on the subject."

My jaw dropped, and my eyes grew wide as I reached for her arm. Holding on to her, I began laughing so hard that I couldn't stand up. When the laughter became contagious, I brought us both tumbling to the ground as Spirit ran back and forth, planting kisses on our faces. We were hysterical with laughter as we lay on the soft grass, trying to catch our breath. Spirit sat panting between us, entangled in love, laughter, and his leash.

"I found a dog-training book today." I turned my head toward her and smiled.

"Perfect timing," she said as she watched the clouds drift by. "I made brownies," she offered, never shifting her gaze from the sky. Then, with a very mischievous tone in her voice, she grinned and said, "Race ya!" And off we ran.

A big plate of brownies was waiting on the kitchen table. I didn't realize how hungry I was until I saw them there. Spirit headed straight for his water bowl, and Mom poured two big glasses of milk and then sat down at the table across from me.

"So," she began, as if things were perfectly normal, "how was your day?"

I had just taken a big bite from the brownie, so I looked at her and rolled my eyes before trying to speak.

"You won't believe it, Mom," I said, with brownies all over my teeth. "But it all started when I went to the library to get the dog-training book."

She laughed, finally understanding what all the hilarity was about earlier. Then with both elbows on the table and hands holding up her chin, she gave me her undivided attention.

"Tell me all about it," she said.

We sat there for an hour as I relived each agonizing moment of the day that was now behind me. She listened to every word I said without ever asking me why I did this or that or what I could have been thinking. Every now and then she would let out a "What?" or "No way!" just to assure me she was on my side all the time. Nothing she could have done would have been more important to me at that moment. Everything seemed far less serious now that we were together, and the two of us were soon laughing at how silly the whole ordeal was.

"What shall we do with this young lady?" my mother asked, pretending to be the principal. Then she draped a dish towel over her shoulders and held a wooden spoon in the air like a scepter as she declared, "Off with her head!"

I had completely forgotten about the trouble I'd been in, and I laughed so hard that milk came out of my nose. Then we laughed some more. I was almost too tired to climb into bed that night, but something popped into my mind just before she turned out the light.

"Mom, Mr. Rubello said something today that was really strange."

"Just one thing?" my mother asked sarcastically.

I thought her comment was funny, but I was too tired to even giggle, so I gave her a little smile to let her know I got her joke.

"So, what did His Highness say?"

"Well, it was when I first went into his office. He was looking at my file, and he said I was one of the better students at school."

"Point for the principal," she said with a smirk.

"Yeah, but then he said I was also one of the more privileged. What do you think he meant by that?"

The shock that registered on my mother's face was off the charts and was followed by an equally alarming look of sheer rage.

"He said what?" she shot back at me, not waiting for a reply. "Why, that little weasel. If I ever get my hands on him, so help me—"

"Mom!" I said loudly, bringing her back to her senses.

"I'm sorry, honey. That man just makes my blood boil!"

"I know, Mom. But the thing is, he was kind of mad when he said it. I really don't know what he meant by 'privileged.' Do you think Mr. Rubello thinks we're rich because of where we live?"

The rage on my mother's face slowly turned to sorrow as I continued.

"That would make sense," I said, ignoring her discomfort. "I mean, it's not as if where we live is a secret. I guess if I weren't me, I'd think I was rich too." This made my mother smile. "But what I don't get is…why would he be mad about it?"

"I don't know, kiddo," she said sincerely. "Not knowing the truth can make people jump to the wrong conclusions. And I guess in our case, it makes them jealous."

"It still doesn't make any sense. Just because he thinks we're rich—even though we aren't—shouldn't make him mad, even if it does make him jealous."

"He's not mad because he thinks we're rich, Lily. He's mad because he thinks we don't deserve it."

The idea that anyone might be jealous of me made me very uncomfortable. How was I supposed to deal with something that was unspoken?

"Mom, do you think my friends are jealous?"

My mother's thoughtful words said, "Of course not."

But her face said, "Absolutely."

CHAPTER 8

OFF WITH HER HEAD

W e were halfway through breakfast when my mother announced that she was going to call Principal Rubello to discuss what had happened the day before. I was suddenly sick to my stomach.

"Aw, Mom, do you have to? I don't want to make a big deal of it. School's almost over, and everyone will forget about it. Can we just let it go? Please?"

"I don't think so, honey. If I don't contact him, he might assume I don't care about what happens at school. Nothing could be further from the truth. I promise I won't make a big deal of it. I will be very calm and polite. But it's important that we speak up when we believe we have been treated unfairly. Do you understand?"

I stared at my breakfast with my face buried in my fists.

"Lily?"

"Yes, I understand." But I dreaded what would come of the day.

We barely spoke as we walked under the shelter of the elms to the bus stop. I grumbled, and Mom stood her ground, while Spirit walked happily in front of us with the leash clenched between his teeth.

"He thinks he's walking us," my mother said, chuckling, while I continued to pout. As the bus rolled slowly toward my stop, she assured me everything would be fine.

"Nothing to worry about," she insisted.

"That's what Mrs. Olson said," I mumbled as I lumbered toward the bus.

The door opened. Mr. Little gave me a quick smile as he waved to my mother. It seemed unusually quiet as I stepped onto the bus, especially for a Friday morning. Ordinarily there would be lots of chatter and laughter as the year-end excitement became more and more difficult to contain. But everyone was seemingly preoccupied or talking quietly with their heads down.

What was going on? Did someone die? I sat down next to Maddie, who was staring out the window again.

"Hi, Maddie," I said as I did every morning.

"Hi" came her reply. But she didn't look at me.

The ride to school felt very strange, and then I found myself walking to my class alone. This had never happened before. Maddie and I had always walked together until we got to her classroom, which was just down the hall from mine, and then we'd say, "Bye! See ya after school!" And that's how we'd start our days.

But on this morning, she disappeared as soon as we stepped off the bus, and even though I looked around, she was nowhere to be found. About half the class was in the room when I arrived, so I quietly made my way to my desk.

Billy Gabershevski was clowning around, as usual, but stopped throwing spit balls across the room long enough to say, "Oh, look whose back. Little Miss Perfect! Ha-ha! Looks like you're not so perfect after all."

The boys who were the targets for his saliva-soaked paper wads hooted as I walked to my seat.

"Woo-hoo! The Queen of Perfect is back in town," Billy Gabershevski said, and the paper-wad kids laughed.

"What's their problem?" I snarled to myself.

Things were nearly out of control, with spitballs and erasers flying through the air by the time Mr. Wicket walked in. The particularly foul mood that he arrived with was only exacerbated by the turbulent atmosphere in the classroom. Slamming his briefcase down on his desk, he clapped his hands together and shouted, "That will be enough!" The room was still. "I don't want to hear a single word from any of you for the rest of the day. You will speak only when you are spoken to *by me*. Is that clear?"

Everyone, including Billy Gabershevski, said, "Yes, Mr. Wicket."

We stood as we recited the Pledge of Allegiance, and everyone remained silent as the morning announcements were made over the school intercom. We were about to lift our history books out of our desktops when Mr. Wicket advised that we were going to take a pop quiz on the Civil War. There were several groans from Billy Gabershevski and his crew, to which Mr. Wicket responded by tapping his ruler loudly on the desk.

"Silence! Put your books and papers away this instant. I want to see nothing more than a single number-two pencil on the desk in front of you." He pulled a stack of papers from his briefcase and walked to the first row of desks by the window.

"The quiz is to remain facedown until everyone in the class has received a copy and I have given you permission to turn it over. Anyone who looks at the quiz before being instructed to do so will receive an automatic zero, which will affect fifteen percent of your overall grade."

A few gasps were heard throughout the room as he handed the packets to the first person in each row. He kept his eyes on the class to ensure no one tried to catch a glimpse of what was awaiting us. When every quiz had been passed out, he stood in front of the class. "You may turn over your papers." Glancing at the clock, he announced, "The quiz begins...now."

I printed my name and the date at the top of the page before reading the first question. It was much easier than I expected, and I breathed a sigh of relief. The questions became more difficult as the quiz went on, which made me nervous, but I made it through without blanking out, which had happened in the past.

I always got good grades, which surprised me since I usually felt like I was flying by the seat of my pants. But my mother assured me that I was very smart and that all I needed was confidence. The night before a test was always gruelling because something would switch off in my head before I was finished studying, and I couldn't focus on anything, which freaked me out. It never seemed to bother my mother, though. She told me that all the information was tucked away in the back of my brain and would come to the front when I needed it. Her words didn't stop me from worrying, even though she was usually right. On this day,

I appeared to be fully prepared for the Civil War. What I wasn't prepared for was lunch.

By the time the bell rang for lunch, I had forgotten about all the weirdness that happened on the bus and during class. I was getting quite hungry and hoped there was something delicious being served in the cafeteria. It wasn't often that my mother allowed me to buy lunch, as it became too expensive. But she had no time to prepare something for me this morning, so I picked up a tray and stood in line to check out the specials for the day. I surveyed the steaming trays behind the glass-domed serving station where the women in plastic bonnets and gloves stood poised to place precise nutritional portions onto plates.

"I'm not really in the mood for a hot lunch," I thought. "Though the green beans and ham look good."

I smiled at the women as I moved toward the salad bar. One of the kitchen workers had just delivered a clean stack of plates that came straight from the dishwasher. The dish was still hot when I picked it up, which startled me. I nearly dropped it on the floor.

"Whoa!" I said loudly. And I heard a few giggles from behind me.

The vegetables and fruits looked very fresh, and I piled the food onto my plate—romaine, cucumbers, tomatoes, grated cheese, sunflower seeds, hard-boiled eggs, raisins, and a few strawberries on the side. I topped my salad off with a scoop of creamy Caesar dressing and then filled a cup with water from the soda dispenser before getting in the checkout line.

The woman at the cash register was someone I had seen nearly every school day since I started kindergarten. She was a black woman with short, straight hair that appeared to be glued down to keep the natural curl from springing up unexpectedly. Her smile was genuinely warm and always worth returning, although she didn't give smiles away easily or often.

She had a real knack for sizing people up very quickly. She could also build you up or cut you down with just a glance, which was something I considered to be a powerful gift. It was as though she knew everything about you the very first time she saw you. I think she was right just about all the time. Her name was Isabella, but everyone called her Izzy. Izzy didn't like wise guys or smart alecks, and she had no time for the popular kids who thought they were too cool to say hello. I could never understand why anyone would waste an opportunity to make Izzy smile, especially when all they gained was a puffed-up sense of superiority.

"Some people take pleasure in believing they are better than others," my mother once told me.

She was right. As for me, I'd take Izzy's happy grin over a lifetime of cool any day of the week. I was very glad to see her on this otherwise unusual day.

"Hi, Izzy," I said as I arrived at her register. "How are you today?"

But she didn't smile back.

"Well, good afternoon, Miss Lily. I'm just fine, thank you." She tilted her head and looked right through me. I felt like she was sizing me up, and it made me very uncomfortable. "But I should be asking you, how are *you* today?"

I glanced around to see if she might be speaking to someone else.

"I'm okay," I said nervously.

"Are you now? Because I hear you've been spending some time with the man in the office instead of in the classroom where you belong."

I was stunned. I leaned over my tray and whispered, "How do you know about that?"

"News gets around, little one." She took hold of my wrist as she handed me my change and said, "Be a good girl... understand? There ain't nothin' more important than your education!"

Then she winked at me. But she still didn't smile.

"Yes, ma'am. Thank you." I had a hollow feeling in my stomach as I walked in a daze toward the table where I'd sat with my friends for the past four years. But when I got there, there wasn't a chair for me to sit in.

"Where's my seat?" I asked.

Lisa Leiber glanced over her shoulder. "Oh, sorry, Lil. No room! I guess you'll have to find another table."

Another table? What other table? There wasn't another empty seat in the whole lunchroom, at least not with anyone I knew. I stood there for a long time as my friends shifted their seats and ignored me. Every eye seemed to glance at me and then quickly turn away as chairs were adjusted to ensure there wasn't a place for me to fit in. I spotted a table in the back of the room with only three girls and a very skinny boy, so I walked over and gestured toward one of the empty chairs and asked, "Is anyone sitting here?"

"Doesn't look like it," the girl with black wavy hair said to her sandwich.

I put my tray down as far away from the others as possible. I pretended not to notice the people I was sitting with, although they all seemed to be staring at me. I unwrapped the flatware from the napkin and placed the napkin on my lap.

A sizable portion of salad was about to enter my mouth when the black-haired girl asked, "Aren't you the girl who got into so much trouble yesterday?"

The fork froze in front of me. "Excuse me?" I asked, hoping I didn't hear what I thought she just said.

"I heard that one of the smart kids was sent to Rubello's office for the whole afternoon. Was that you?"

"Well," I said, not wanting to lie, "I did go to Mr. Rubello's office yesterday. Yes. I did."

"Wow. That's amazing."

"Yeah," said the skinny boy, "Amazing!"

"I don't know what's so amazing about it. It wasn't something I planned." I knew I was being rude, but this whole incident was starting to get on my nerves. I took the bite of salad.

"No," said another girl with braces and an orange headband. "I totally get it. No one ever plans stuff like that."

The girl who hadn't yet spoken snorted really loudly, which startled me, but as it turned out, that was just the way she laughed.

"It's just," the braces girl said, "well, it's just that smart kids never get into trouble, even when they do something wrong. Everybody looks the other way or makes excuses for them."

"Yeah," said the black-haired girl. "And the cool kids get away with stuff all the time. Somebody's gonna get blamed for what they did. It's just not gonna be them."

"Yeah," everyone else said in agreement.

I looked down as I took a sip of water and then stuck the fork into the middle of my salad a couple of times before taking another bite.

"So you must have done something really bad," the braces girl decided.

"Yeah," added the skinny boy. "It must've been really bad."

I continued to eat without looking up, until the braces girl broke the silence and asked, "So what did you do?"

I took a deep breath and held it. I almost didn't answer. "I broke a rule," I said solemnly.

"No way!" the black-haired girl gasped, seemingly impressed.

"On purpose?" the braces girl asked.

I looked at her without saying a word. I was growing tired of defending myself over something so minor that was, after all, no one else's business. In retrospect, not responding was probably the worst thing I could have done, as they immediately assumed that silence equaled guilt. A seed was planted that day that I would remember forever.

CHAPTER 9

A DISAPPOINTMENT
TO EVERYONE

"Hi, sunshine," my mother called out cheerfully as I dragged my backpack off the bus. "Oh my heavens! What in the world is the matter?" she asked as she grabbed my burden and slung it over her shoulder.

I shuffled silently down the road, frowning at the ground. Mother kept pace and never took her eyes from me, waiting, I suppose, for a response. "Okay," she said before changing the subject. "But this is no way to start the weekend."

The weekend! Thank heavens! I wouldn't have to go back to that horrible school for two whole days.

"I was thinking," she segued expertly, "that this might be the perfect time to take Spirit out on the lake. We haven't had the boat out yet, and I'm sure he's ready for it. In fact, I'll bet he would have a blast. What do you think?"

Spirit tugged on my shoestring for attention, which nearly made me fall.

"Spirit!" I barked at the dog as I yanked my foot away from him. I was a bit rougher than I meant to be, which startled everyone.

"Lily!" my mother scolded.

She quickly picked Spirit up and cradled him in her arms to protect him from big, bad me. Her reaction seemed a little extreme, as though she was intentionally trying to make me feel guilty. Mission accomplished. I gave them both a sideward glance and then turned my attention back to myself.

"Something happened at school today," she guessed accurately. "Did Rubello give you a hard time? Because if he did…so help me—"

"No!" I snapped back at her. "It was nothing like that. I didn't even see him all day."

She waited for me to elaborate as we continued walking toward the cottage, but I kept my sights set straight ahead of me and locked my lips with a frown. The silence was killing her.

"So…what was it then?"

My blood was nearly at its boiling point when she held Spirit up like a ventriloquist's dummy and said in a silly voice, "Please tell us what's wrong, Lily. You're making us very sad. You don't want us to be sad, do you?"

My mother had that long, sorrowful look on her face as she assumed the role of a talking dog. Spirit, on the other hand, didn't have a clue as to what was going on, and he bounced goofily along, with his tongue hanging out of his mouth. I tried not to laugh, but they looked so cute that I couldn't help but soften.

"Argh!" I growled, not knowing where to begin. "I don't know what's wrong. Nothing. Everything! The entire day was a disaster. For some reason, none of my friends would talk to me, and I had to sit with some really weird kids at lunch who just wanted to talk about the trouble I'd gotten into." I kicked a stone that lay innocently in my path.

"That's the problem with small towns," my mother muttered. "People get their noses in everyone else's business."

"I mean…I don't even know those kids," I grumbled as she shook her head. "But what's up with my friends? Why is everyone ignoring me? It's like I have head lice or something. I mean…even Maddie gave me the cold shoulder. I might as well have been invisible."

"Maddie? Really? I'm surprised."

"I know! She even bolted off the bus this morning just so she wouldn't have to walk with me to class."

"Hmmm. If I had to make a guess," my mother said knowingly, "I would say that the news of you going to the principal's office must've traveled quickly. When the parents got wind of it, they might have warned their kids not to be seen with you. At least until this all blows over. Smart kids never get into trouble, you know."

"That's what the braces girl said."

"The who?" she asked curiously.

"Nobody. Just one of the girls I had to have lunch with today. She said smart kids never get into trouble because people look the other way. And cool kids never get caught, but somebody always gets blamed for the stuff they do." I stopped to think about that for a moment. "Do you think she was talking about them? Do you think that the cool kids set up the outcast kids to take the fall when they do something bad?"

"I wouldn't doubt it," my mother replied.

"That really stinks. I can't believe I never knew that."

"Because you aren't cool or outcast."

"Thanks…I think," I said, not knowing how to take her comment.

"I just meant that it shouldn't be important to you."

"I really wish I noticed stuff like that," I said, feeling genuinely sorry for the kids I had lunch with.

"Why would you? You're too busy learning, to pay attention to things that amount to absolutely nothing. Like who's cool. And who's outcast."

"No. I notice who's cool. You can't help it. They're always in groups, and everyone pays so much attention to them because they have great hair and really nice clothes."

"Not exactly redeeming qualities."

"Yeah," I said, kicking another stone. "I kind of wish I could hang out with them sometimes, though. It looks like fun."

"Lily, you're only twelve years old. You're smart, kind, funny, and much wiser than most of those kids will ever be. We can't be measured by the clothes we wear or the people we hang out with. Please don't worry about being anyone but the wonderful you that you already are. You have a lot to be grateful for. And I don't ever want you to become one of those people who spends so much time thinking about what they don't have that they forget to be thankful for all they do have."

Spirit barked as if he was in complete agreement, but I had a tough time being grateful for a really lousy day. I knew my mom would be disappointed in me if I didn't let things go. So I took Spirit from her arms and said, "I'm very thankful for you, my wonderful Spirit!" There was anticipation all over my mother's face as I nuzzled my nose in Spirit's fur, then added, "I love you too, Mom."

"I'll never grow tired of hearing it," she said, wearing a full-on grin.

We had an early dinner that night, then Mom and I took Spirit for a walk through the woods. Over the years we had carved out a path by clearing the twigs and brush until we made a perfect trail. It took us past the pond and through an open field that wound its way through the woods to a babbling brook. We searched for large, flat rocks near the stream one summer and placed them in the water as stepping stones to the woods on the other side. After passing over the brook, the path split in two. The path on the left circled back toward another field that led to the house, while the one to the right went to the lake.

I was very apprehensive about taking Spirit toward the lake, even if he was on a leash. I didn't want him to become too familiar with that part of the property, as it was protected only by evergreens and a split rail fence. It was the farthest point from the house, which was barely visible through the trees; and several signs served as warnings to potential trespassers. But the lake was a popular summer attraction, and the signs seemed to draw out-of-towners to the property rather than steer them away from it. The thought that Spirit might run under the fence was an ongoing concern, and the irrational fear that he could be stolen or, worse yet, hit by a car haunted me. I anticipated reaching the split in the path long before we got there, and I decided I would get us safely on the road home and avoid the lake for as long as possible. Spirit loved exploring, and after we found our way to the open field by the house, Mother thought it would be fun to see how he handled a little freedom and removed his leash.

"What if we lose sight of him?" I protested. "He could get lost or something worse!"

"He's just a puppy, Lil. He can't run that fast yet. We'll keep a close eye on him. Look! He's got the scent of something already."

Spirit rooted through the thick underbrush with his nose to the ground as he darted back and forth, then lifted his head to catch sight of where the smell had gone. He stood frozen for a moment and then put his nose to the ground again. Suddenly, a rabbit leapt through the tall grass, with Spirit running right after him.

"Spirit!" I yelled in a panic.

"He's fine," my mother said, grabbing my arm to keep me from darting after him. "The rabbit will outrun him soon, and he'll turn around. Just watch."

My heart was pounding. Sure enough, the rabbit took off across the field as Spirit stood perfectly still. He let out a few barks that were intended to be howls, then turned around to see where we were.

"Spirit!" I yelled again as I clapped my hands maniacally to get his attention. "Come on, boy! Come on!"

Spirit pranced toward us. He seemed quite full of himself, as if his mission had been to chase that rabbit off his field. My mother laughed, and I let out a loud sigh of relief.

"See? I told you he'd come back. He's a good dog."

We both praised and patted him as he sat panting happily between us.

It was time to head back to the house, and even though there was still plenty of light outside, my thoughts were on climbing into bed. The past two days had been physically and emotionally draining, and I was struggling to keep my eyes open. Mom ran a nice, hot bubble bath, and I soaked for at least twenty minutes while she cleaned up the dishes, turned down the sheets, and brought in my pajamas along with a freshly laundered towel.

"You're going to turn into a prune." She held out the towel and motioned for me to get out of the tub.

"Ah, it feels so good! I don't want to get out."

"Come on, kiddo. The water must be getting cold by now. If it's not, it will be. And all the bubbles will be gone. Might as well jump into this nice, fluffy towel while it's still a little warm. I just took it out of the dryer."

My ears perked up. I was a warm-towel kind of kid any time of the year. So, I stepped out of the tub and onto the thick, shaggy rug as bubbles ran down my belly and legs. Mom wrapped the towel around me, and I buried my face in it before drying off.

"Mmm!" I said, taking another whiff of sheer cotton bliss. "It smells like lemongrass."

"Good nose," she said, clearly impressed. "I just bought a new detergent this week and tried it for the first time today. I like the scent, but it's a little expensive. I think we'll just use it on the linens."

"I could smell it all day," I said, moving my nose to a not-yet-smelled spot.

"Well, you'll have to save some of the fragrance for later. Right now, you need to put on your pajamas and brush your teeth. We still have to get through that hair before you hit the hay, and your eyes are barely open."

I yawned and shook my head in agreement as I stole one last sniff before slipping into my pajamas. I climbed into bed, and Mother sat next to me and gently brushed the hair from my eyes.

"Are you too tired to hear more of Mira's story?" she asked.

"The girl without a reflection? I thought about her today as we were walking through the woods," I lied.

"Did you really?" She seemed genuinely surprised and happy. "That's when I thought about her too!"

"Wow, what a coincidence!" I said, hoping my smile didn't appear too fake.

She clearly wanted to continue the story, but I wasn't in the mood to hear about perfect little Mira and her perfect little life, which had everything mine didn't: two parents, a grandmother, and entire towns that adored her. People always stopped by just to be with her family, while we never had visitors. Even my friends weren't allowed to come over because it wasn't our house, which was something else Mira had that I didn't. Her own house. Her own house on her own hill, for heaven's sake! It was starting to depress me.

But I didn't want to hurt my mother's feelings, so I said, "I really want to hear more of the story, Mom. But not tonight, okay? I don't think I can stay awake another minute. And that wouldn't be fair to Mira."

She smiled as she tucked me in.

"You're very wise." She turned off the light. "This has been a long week. And there'll always be another day for the story. Right?"

I nodded, but as things turned out…we were both wrong.

CHAPTER 10

THE PROBLEM WITH OTTERHOUNDS

Mother had been up for hours by the time I stumbled downstairs for breakfast.

"Good morning," she said, absorbed in something she was reading.

"Hey," I mumbled, not fully awake. "Where's Spirit?"

"Outside," she said, gesturing with her hand.

"You put him outside?" I cried out and bolted toward the door.

"Calm down!" she yelled. "He's on the leash."

The screen door slammed behind me as I ran into the yard with my heart suddenly in my throat. Having paid no attention to my mother's words of assurance, I was surprised to find Spirit resting peacefully under the maple tree.

"Spirit!" I shouted, shattering his contentedness.

He sprung to his feet at the sound of my voice and instinctively ran toward me. The leash yanked him backward, which prompted a blood-curdling yelp. The sound was like an alarm going off in my brain, alerting me to the danger that lie ahead. At that moment, I thought he needed to be rescued and believed that I alone could save him. I sprinted across the yard to the tree, where I fell to my knees as Spirit pressed his dirty paws against my pajama top and happily licked my face.

"It's okay, Spirit! It's okay," I repeated soberly, as if I'd just delivered him from a terrible fate.

Mother had been standing behind me as the drama unfolded. I didn't have to turn around to know she had her hands planted firmly on her hips as she shook her head in disbelief.

"See?" she said, as though nothing traumatic had just happened. "I told you he was fine."

It was beyond me how she could think that what she did was fine, and I buried my face in Spirit's fur before giving her a scowling look.

"No thanks to you," I said to myself, as I clung to my tethered Spirit.

"So," she said, sitting cross-legged on the grass, "breakfast first, a quick shower, then a walk by the lake. How does that sound?"

I was still mad at her for something she hadn't done and not fully over my irrational snit, so I decided to ignore her. Spirit abandoned my lap for hers as soon as she was on the ground, and I wanted to give them both a very nasty look.

"Sit!" she commanded.

To my surprise, he sat. She praised him for being a good dog and gently rubbed behind his ear, which calmed him down immediately. Soon he was lying next to her with his head on her leg. I couldn't believe it. She was the one who tied him to a tree while I was the one who saved him. His head should be on my lap, not hers.

"Humph," I grunted a bit more loudly than I'd intended. I was sure Mother heard me, but she pretended she didn't.

"So, what do you think?" she asked again. "Breakfast, a quick shower, and a walk to the lake? It's a perfect day for it."

"What were you reading?" I asked, although I wasn't really interested.

"Oh, it's a book I found on rare dog breeds. There's a piece about otterhounds in it. It's very interesting. Did you know they were originally from Great Britain?"

"Yes," I answered indignantly.

"Well, it says the breed dates back to the twelfth century and that there are fewer than eight hundred otterhounds worldwide today. They are rarer than the Giant Panda! Can you imagine that?"

"I can. Because Mrs. Robbins already told us that."

"She didn't tell us they were rarer than the Giant Panda," my mother said defensively.

"It has to say something more than that. Does it say anything about how smart they are? Or what they like to do? Does it say anything about *training* them?"

"Training them? Well, yes. Yes, it does say something about training them," she stammered. "But not much more than the book you got from the library." She tapped the side of her head with her finger as if the book she read moments ago was stuck there, refusing to come out. Something was up. She was keeping information from me, and I didn't like it one bit.

"Hmm," she said, still dancing around the subject. "Let's see…it said that they're very rugged and need a lot of exercise. Oh, and that they love to swim! So, he's going to go crazy when he sees the pond." She seemed genuinely excited about this piece of news, when all I could imagine was Spirit struggling in the middle of the pond and no way to help him.

"When he's older," I warned her. "He's too little to go in the pond now."

"Maybe," she said, without giving up. "But he's not exactly a small dog even if he is just a puppy. And it's an instinct, after all. We can't suppress it forever. I don't see any reason why he can't go in the pond."

Had she lost her mind? Why were we having such a futile discussion? Whether she liked it or not…Spirit was *my* dog. And I wasn't ready for him to go in the pond. Not now. And maybe not ever.

"Right," she said. "Well, I guess we'll just have to see. Anyway, otterhounds love water. Any water! It doesn't matter if it's in a pond, a puddle, or a bowl. If there's water around…he's going to find it. So don't be surprised if he tries to dunk his whole head in his water dish!"

The image of Spirit's head submerged in his water bowl made me laugh, and I lightened up for the first time all morning. I took a deep breath and let my whole body relax when I exhaled. It was a good feeling, and I wished I'd done it sooner.

"What else does it say about them?" I asked, this time with sincere interest.

Mother's face brightened up, and her voice was suddenly cheery. "Well…they're very, *very* friendly. But they're also reserved. So, they make good watchdogs but not good guard dogs."

"That's okay," I said, nodding in approval, and I mentally checked off one thing from my list as my mother smiled.

"Yep!" she said. "That's just fine!" She looked to the clouds for more fun facts about the rare, friendly, water-loving otterhounds and snapped her fingers when she got one. "And," she said with too much enthusiasm, "they're clumsy. So, they aren't very safe around toddlers."

I crinkled my nose and shrugged my shoulders. "We don't have any toddlers," I added.

"No, we don't," she affirmed. And I checked off another thing from my list.

"They're friendly, happy, and very loyal," she said.

"What about obedient? What does it say about how obedient they are?"

"Well"—she rolled her eyes upward as if the answer was floating in thin air—"it describes them as having a 'mind of their own.'"

"What does that mean?" I squinted one eye as I gazed at her, wondering why she was so hesitant.

"It means they can be stubborn as well as a little slow in learning—not because they're stupid but because they have set their minds on something other than what their trainer wants them to do. So, we're going to have to be very patient and strong-willed in training him."

I mulled over what she'd just said and decided it was confirmation of something I'd already suspected. In some way it was comforting to know my instincts were right. And I accepted the challenge of patiently yet lovingly training my Spirit to yield to my will.

She brought up going to the lake again, but I wanted nothing to do with it. She thought it would be fun for the three of us to go out on the fishing boat, but I had a mile-long list as to why that was a bad idea.

"Otterhounds love water," I began. "What if he jumps overboard?"

"He's not going to jump overboard, but if you're concerned, we'll keep him on his leash."

"We can't do that. It would be cruel. He'll think we're really mean."

"I doubt that."

"What if he gets sick when we're out in the middle of the lake?" I pressed on.

"Why would he get sick?"

"I don't know. Dogs can get sick, can't they? What if he got sick in the boat and threw up? That would be a major mess."

My mother shook her head. She hadn't given up on the idea of spending the day on the lake, but she was clearly tired of arguing about it. "Why don't you go get dressed, and we can figure out what we're going to do afterward. If we keep sitting here talking about it, the day will be gone, and we will have done nothing with it."

I didn't think that was such a bad idea, at this point, as I would have preferred doing nothing over losing Spirit in the lake. I took my sweet time getting ready and even took a shower unnecessarily. My mother was in the yard pulling weeds from our little flower garden, and Spirit was laying beneath the tree. She had added several feet to his freedom by tying a length of clothesline to the leash, so he wasn't as confined. But the experience of nearly being choked to death the last time he saw me come toward him in the yard must have been fresh in his mind, as he sat up and wagged his tail instead of running to meet me.

My mother looked up from her gardening and said, "You look very nice," which I interpreted as, "What took you so long?"

"Thanks," I replied under my breath.

"Your dog needs some exercise," she said, digging at a particularly stubborn dandelion. "Why don't you take him for a walk?"

"By myself?" I asked, half surprised, half miffed.

"Sure! You can handle it. I want to get a little more work done before I start thinking about lunch." I suspected this was just another way of reminding me about the time I'd spent getting ready and decided it would be wise to put some distance between us.

"Well, okay. If you say so."

I untied Spirit's leash from the rope, put the loop on my wrist, and grabbed it with both hands as he jumped up and down excitedly. "We won't be long," I called out to my mother.

"Take your time," she said, pretending not to watch as I held on to Spirit for dear life.

The grass had been freshly mowed in the field just behind the barn, so I decided it was the safest place to walk. Spirit pulled me in the direction of the meadow, but I knew plenty of rabbits were hiding in the tall grass. I tugged on his leash and said sternly, "No, Spirit! This way!" It took several forceful tugs before he gave up and turned his attention to the open field before him.

He seemed happy to be away from the tree and pranced through the grass like a Clydesdale in a parade. I was beginning to feel a little less worried about losing him and a little more interested in just being with him. Soon I was comfortable enough for us to run together, although I made sure I kept a tight grip on his leash. I tried to keep pace with him, but I knew I was holding him back. He wanted to explore the acres of land that stretched out before him, but the inconceivable notion that he might somehow get away from me overpowered my desire to let him run free. I thought about what to do for a second and then decided, "Safety first!" I picked him up and turned back through familiar ground to the secure confines of home.

My mother was in the same spot in the garden as when we left. She glanced up at us briefly and then turned her attention back to the weeds. "That was quick," she affirmed, as we walked toward her.

I sensed disappointment in her voice, and it agitated me. After all, this was the first time I'd ventured out alone with Spirit, and although I was fully aware that it was my anxiety that prevented us from a more meaningful adventure, I expected a hero's welcome.

"Yeah, well, I think Spirit is thirsty. I'm going to give him some water."

I didn't want to be around her, so I took Spirit in the house and hoped she wouldn't follow me inside. She didn't. And that made me angry. I sat at the kitchen table with my cheek buried in my fist and frowned at the floor. I heard her enter through the laundry room door, and her sudden presence startled Spirit, who had fallen asleep on his quilted bed. He yapped a few times before realizing it was her and then wiggled and waggled, trying hard to get her attention. She washed her hands as she looked down at the excited pup, assuring him she'd get to him in a second. A sound came from him that was not quite a cry but not quite a yelp, and it begged her to "hurry up and pet me." She giggled as she dried off her hands, then sat cross-legged on the floor, with Spirit jumping to wash her face with kisses. Seeing how happy he was, put me in a lousier mood than I was already in, and I turned away from the playful scene with a snarl plastered on my face. My mother showed signs of growing tired of my mood.

"What in the world is the matter with you today, Lily?"

What did she want me to say? That nothing was going right in my life, and now my dog liked her better than me and it was making me really mad and really jealous?

"Nothing," I grumbled. "What's the matter with you?"

My words left a sour taste in my mouth the moment I spoke them, and my arrogance made me grimace. Unfortunately, I was too self-absorbed to pay attention to my mother's expression, which had turned from concern to anger. My behavior was not only shocking, it was hurtful and completely unacceptable. And for the first time in my entire life, my mother didn't try to comfort or console me.

Instead, she said, "I think it might be best for everyone if you went to your room."

"Fine!" I fired back, without looking at her.

The dishes rattled in the cabinet as I stomped through the kitchen and up the stairs. Then I slammed my bedroom door. The idea that my mother and my dog were having the time of their lives together while I was now stuck in my room infuriated me. I was sure they weren't even giving me a single thought, so I was determined not to think of them either. I huffed and stewed as I paced around my room, looking for something to do that was better than whatever they were doing.

"I'll read!" I declared out loud. "They can be as stupid as they want. See if I care."

Staring at the bookshelf, my eyes couldn't focus on a single title. I pulled a book out of its space, looked at the cover, then threw it on the floor. Then I pulled another book out, looked at it, and threw it on the floor. I did this with every single book until the entire shelf was empty and the floor was full. Disgusted with life and the mess I made, I flopped onto my bed and frowned at the ceiling. I was lying in bed, fuming, when the kitchen door slammed, and I heard my mother calling out to Spirit.

"Come on, boy," she said. "Come on!" Then I heard her laugh as she praised him. "Good boy, Spirit!"

"Oh great," I said to myself. "She probably doesn't even have him on a leash."

The thought of Spirit enjoying my mother's company more than mine was still brewing when I said, "Fine! Let him run away. Then she'll be sorry."

I clutched a vaporous lifeline of pride when the possibility that I might be right terrified me. I jumped out of bed and searched for them through my bedroom window, but they were nowhere in sight. My heart began pounding so loudly, I thought it would come out of my chest. And I broke into a cold sweat as I ran toward my bedroom door.

"Please let him be okay," I pleaded over and over in my head.

I didn't see them when I raced into the yard, and my head began throbbing as more terror set in. Then I heard them on the side of the house and said, "Thank heavens!" as I followed the sound of my mother's voice. My sudden presence came as quite a surprise, especially with the agitated state I was in.

"Excuse me, young lady," my mother said authoritatively, "but who gave you permission to leave your room?"

Her reprimand fell on deaf ears when I saw Spirit walking without his leash. I lunged at him, grabbing him into my arms. I lashed out at my mother, "I knew it! I knew you had him out here without a leash! You don't even care if he runs away!" I held the dog tightly against my chest.

"What in the world are you talking about?" my mother fired back. "What has gotten into you, Lily? He's not going to run away, and even if he tried, he'd wear himself out long before he ever got off the property. You're being completely irrational."

Spirit tried to wiggle free from my grasp, but I restrained him. He began to pant, helplessly, as he waited to be released from the protective custody of my arms. My mother was right. I was behaving irrationally. But I didn't care. Why wasn't she getting it? Why didn't she understand that there were at least a million ways that Spirit could leave Lindenwood and never come back? Why hadn't she considered all the what-ifs that were rattling around in my brain? I just wanted her to agree with me. Was that too much to ask? Seriously! This was my mother! She never let me down before. Why now? Why wasn't she agreeing with me now that my entire world seemed to be falling apart? Everyone at school hated me. I had no friends. I was probably going to fail every one of my classes. And now I had to worry about Spirit running away and getting hit by a car or drowning or being stolen or some other horrible thing. This day was turning into my worst nightmare, and all she could do was tell me I was being irrational.

The power of my fear was suddenly heightened by the overwhelming presence of guilt and humiliation. I searched for a single, valid thought that would bring me back down to earth but found only the sound of my beating heart echoing through my hollow brain. Spirit wiggled wildly and jumped from my arms.

He yelped when he landed, and I heard my mother cry out, "Spirit!" And then, "Lily!"

I stormed into the house and back upstairs to my room, where I flopped down on the bed and wept into my pillow until I had cried myself to sleep.

It was well after dusk when I opened my eyes, and the only light was a dim stream that came from the hall outside my bedroom door. It took a moment to adjust to the darkness, but when I did, I saw my mom sleeping soundly in the chair by my bed and Spirit curled up quietly in the blanket next to me. I wished that I could freeze that moment and stay in it forever. Lying in the stillness, soaking in the sound of each quiet breath, my eyes closed once again, and I drifted off to sleep in peace.

CHAPTER 11

THE TWELFTH DAY OF JUNE

The school year was about to end, and as far as I was concerned, it couldn't come fast enough. The episode with Principal Rubello had turned my life upside down, and I was struggling with everything from schoolwork to lunch. My friends continued to act weird, and I didn't feel welcome at their table, so I ate with the outcast kids every day. They were actually very nice and had a lot of interesting things to say—not to me necessarily. But they didn't seem to mind that I was at their table and paid attention whenever I said something, which wasn't very often. Usually I just listened and smiled or laughed if it was appropriate. I was glad that I had a place to sit where I wasn't completely unwanted. But I had to admit that I felt pretty bad knowing I was one giant step farther away from ever being accepted by the cool kids.

Mom and Spirit hadn't missed a day meeting me at the bus stop since my last major meltdown, but that didn't stop me from worrying until I caught sight of them. The fear of losing Spirit began as soon as I sat down next to Maddie and the bus rolled away. It probably wouldn't have been so bad if Maddie and I were still friends. But I think she was torn between wanting to talk to me and not wanting to make the other girls mad at her, so she kept our conversations as brief as possible without being totally rude. I kind of understood her position. I mean maybe I would act the same way if she were the one who'd been ostracized by everyone, especially Lisa Lieber, who could be really mean when she didn't get her way on absolutely everything. No one dared go against her. I could never understand why anyone liked her. She was very snooty and stuck up, as if she was better than everyone else. The funny thing was that she was the least-smartest girl in the "smart kids" group. But everyone treated her as though she was a queen—mostly because they didn't want to be on her bad side.

The good news was that our year-end exams were behind us and the weekend was ahead. The bad news was that my test scores were bound to be awful, and I was seriously stressing over what that would do to my final grades. I'd had a very difficult time concentrating since the Rubello incident, and I couldn't sleep through the night. I even forgot a few very important homework assignments and had all but abandoned the few chores I had at home. Mom tried to help me stay focused by keeping things as even-keeled as possible. She even stopped talking about taking Spirit on the lake or letting him off the leash, and she took over the responsibility of training him. This only made me worry more, as I was sure he was going to obey her and not me. It wasn't something I was trying to do, but I seemed to spend every waking moment waiting for something bad to happen. My life had become a never-ending cycle of anxiety and fear, and I hoped with all my heart that it would end when summer break began.

"Just twenty-five more minutes," I told myself as I looked at the clock in Mr. Wicket's room. "Then I just have to get through the weekend, and there'll only be two and a half more days until this nightmare will be over."

Mr. Wicket leaned against his desk, listening as the class shared their plans for the summer. He was in a very cheerful mood, knowing this unusual school year would soon end for him as well as his students. But it wasn't over yet.

"Mr. Wicket," came Mrs. Olson's voice over the intercom. "Would you please send Lily Johnson to the office? It's not an emergency, but she should bring her backpack with her."

Mr. Wicket walked over to the intercom and pushed a button before speaking. "Will do, Mrs. Olson. She's on her way." He quickly wrote out a hall pass as everyone in the class muttered and stared at me.

"What's she done this time?" I heard Billy Gabershevski laugh above the din.

"That's enough, Mr. Gabershevski. Unless you'd like a hall pass to the principal's office, too." Mr. Wicket was much kinder when he handed me the pass this time. "I'm sure it's nothing to worry about, Lily. We'll see you on Monday. Have a good weekend." Then he gave me a halfhearted smile before turning everyone's attention back to the vacation that was just two and a half days and twenty-three minutes away.

I walked quickly through the halls, certain something must be wrong at home.

I tried to figure out why I had been called to Rubello's office, but I couldn't come up with a single thing. It didn't make sense. I hadn't been late. I hadn't needed a hall pass.

The book! I forgot to return the book!

Miss Finch was standing by Mrs. Olson's desk when I burst through the door. Her arms were folded tightly across her chest, and she had a strange smirk on her face. She didn't say a word to me as I handed the pass to Mrs. Olson who said, "Everything's okay, Lily. Nothing is wrong at home. Nothing to be concerned about. Mr. Rubello just needs to speak with you. It should only take a minute." Miss Finch gloated as I walked past her toward Principal Rubello's office, and Mrs. Olson gave her a very nasty look, which she ignored. "Just give it a little knock," she said sweetly when I arrived at the closed door. "He's expecting you."

I only had to rap on the door once before I was beckoned in by the principal, who was not at all happy to see me. In fact, he was already very, very mad. "You don't need to sit, Miss Johnson. What I have to say to you won't take long."

I immediately felt the need to confess and hoped it would make a difference in his mood. "I know I forgot to return the library book, Mr. Rubello. I didn't do it on purpose, and I'm really sorry. I promise I'll have it on Miss Finch's counter first thing Monday morning with the two-day fine."

Something I said set him off, and his reaction was far from what I'd hoped for.

"Miss Finch," he snorted, "is irrelevant. But rules are rules. I would have thought you'd have learned your lesson from this one."

"Yes, sir. I did learn my lesson. And I'm terribly sorry. Things have been a bit topsy-turvy lately. I'm not sure if I forgot to return the book or if I just forgot what day it is.

But I won't forget again. I promise." My apology fell on deaf ears.

"So, you're telling me you don't have the book?"

"No, sir. I don't have the book."

The fire in his eyes was blazing as he slammed his hand on the desk. "There cannot possibly be an excuse for not returning this particular book, Miss Johnson. I find it inconceivable that you would fly in the face of my authority and take the entire matter of obeying rules so lightly."

I once again was left without a single clue as to why Mr. Rubello was unreasonably angry over something so minor. Then I remembered the comment he'd made about being privileged, and I said something that I wanted to say to him and Maddie and everyone else who mistakenly thought I was rich.

I said, "Mr. Rubello, please! I can bring the book back on Monday, but please don't be mad at me. I'm not rich, Mr. Rubello. You don't have to be jealous because I'm really not rich!"

You could have heard a pin drop. The principal's face turned flaming red as his eyes grew as wide as saucers. He never took them off me as he straightened up very slowly and marched toward me with his hands locked behind his back.

"Jealous?" he asked just above a whisper. His eyebrows were raised as he peered down at me without moving his head. "You think I'm jealous of you, Miss Johnson?" He looked as if he smelled something vile as he strutted in a circle around me like a vulture eyeing his prey. "What do you have that I might be jealous of, Miss Johnson?" He continued walking as he listed the possibilities. "Might I be jealous of the big house you live in? Or the hundreds of acres that sit behind your pretentious iron gate?"

I began to say, "But I don't—"

"Ha! Hardly!"

I froze.

"Or perhaps I should be jealous of the people you own or the way you control them with your threats of destroying their businesses and their very lives."

"But I don't—"

He stopped marching, folded his arms, and leaned toward me with vengeful eyes.

"Of course, *you* don't, Miss Johnson. But I'm not speaking of *you* now, am I? I'm speaking of the very rich, very powerful Myrtle Robbins. The most hated woman in all the world. I'm speaking of the woman who believes she is above the law and above everyone in this town. Just like you believe you are above the rules. The apple doesn't fall far from the tree, does it, Miss Johnson? You are just like her. There is absolutely no difference between you and your grandmother."

"Grandmother?" I said, shaking my head back and forth. "Oh no, Mr. Rubello! Mrs. Robbins isn't my grandmother. She just owns the estate where we live."

"Don't play with me, Miss Johnson. I'm hardly a fool. Do you think I'm the only one in this entire town who isn't aware of who your father was? I can assure you, I am not. Your father was William Robbins, Myrtle Robbins' son. And that, Miss Johnson, makes *you* Myrtle Robbins' granddaughter!"

My eyes searched his for a sign that he was joking. It was surely a horrible misunderstanding. My heart beat loudly in my chest, and I could scarcely breathe as he continued to rant.

"Which explains why you think you can get away with things others must pay for. And why you seem to believe—"

I dropped my backpack and ran toward the door. The principal called after me, as did Mrs. Olson, but the pounding in my head prevented me from hearing them. An icy sensation swept through my veins and poured from my forehead. I felt as though I was running in place as I raced outside toward my bus.

"Miss Johnson!" The principal's voice echoed in my head as I beat against the bus door with my fists.

"Late again, Miss Lily," the driver said.

I stumbled down the narrow aisle to my seat as the bus rolled slowly away. Mr. Rubello waved his arms wildly to get Mr. Little's attention, but the driver had his eyes on the rearview mirror and didn't see him.

"Buckle up, Miss Lily," he said as soon as I slumped into my seat. Then he turned his attention to the road ahead as Mr. Rubello watched the bus drive out of the parking lot.

My hands shook as I pulled the belt across my lap and clicked it into place. The bus rattled and rocked back and forth as it rolled over the speed bump in front of the school. The motion made my stomach churn and sent a cold chill across the back of my neck. I dropped my head into my hands to block the light and prayed that I wouldn't throw up.

"Your father was William Robbins, Myrtle Robbins' son." I heard Rubello's voice in my head and felt everyone's eyes upon me.

"What's wrong with Lily?" someone asked.

"I think she's going to be sick."

"Oh no!" the boy across the aisle cried.

"I hope she waits till she gets home," someone else said.

But the voices were just echoes in the distance, a soundtrack to the horror movie that was repeating in my brain.

"He's lying!" I told myself. "My mother would never hide the most important thing in the world from me."

"And that, Miss Johnson, makes *you* Myrtle Robbins' granddaughter!"

The muscles clenched around my heart as my head fell to my lap. The brakes squealed then whooshed as the bus came to its first stop and was still moving slowly when a few of the boys who sat in the back walked clumsily up the aisle, grabbing the back of people's seats for balance as their backpacks knocked them from side to side. Mr. Little scolded them as they exited, then shut the doors behind them and shifted into gear. The bus jerked as it got up to speed, and the stale air hung over my head, threatening my queasy stomach. The warm rush of wind that blew through the open windows was a welcome relief that came just in time. I sat back in my seat with my eyes still closed and wished my head would stop pounding.

We were nearly at my stop when I heard Maddie say, "Are you okay, Lil?" Her presence startled me, as I'd forgotten she was there. Chills ran through my body as I opened my eyes to the light.

"Maddie," I began, nearly too terrified to speak, "do you know who my grandmother is?"

Maddie looked at me as if I had horns coming out of my head. "Sure. Everyone knows that," she said. The bus slowed down as the brakes squealed and whooshed, bringing it to a stop. "Myrtle Robbins," she said as I stared at her in silence.

"Lily Johnson!" Mr. Little called out. "This is you."

I kept my head down to hide the tears as I ran toward the open door and stepped onto the grass as the bus pulled away. My mind raced with confusion as I stumbled toward the gate that led to Lindenwood. The surroundings suddenly felt completely unfamiliar. I was a stranger in the only home I'd ever known, and I felt bitterly betrayed by the one person in my life I believed I could trust. I needed her to tell me the truth about everything, and I needed her at that very moment. But when I looked for my mother, she wasn't there.

I couldn't feel the ground beneath my feet as I ran through the gates and down the road toward the cottage. My eyes were fixed on the path before me as the landscape blurred around it. Where was she? I felt my heart pounding in my chest as I began to tremble uncontrollably. My mother was nowhere in sight. Wave after wave of fear grabbed hold of me, and I couldn't catch my breath, but this time she wasn't walking toward me. I cried out, desperate to hear her voice. But there was no reply. When I reached the cottage, I opened the kitchen door and saw that the hook where Spirit's leash was kept was empty. "Oh no!" I cried. Where were they?

I stepped into the yard as the screen door slammed behind me, then I stood perfectly still and listened, hoping to hear her voice. But it was quiet. I ran to the field where the path was divided. It was the last place I wanted them to be. I took off down the hill and over the stream where I stopped to catch my breath and listen, but I couldn't hear anything but the thumping in my head.

Then off in the distance, I heard her call out, "Spirit! Spirit! Come on, boy!"

She whistled for him as I ran down and up the little hills, following her voice until I saw her standing in the tall grass by the path that led to the lake. She was startled when she saw me, and I sensed something was wrong. The closer I got to her, the more intense my feeling became.

"Lily!" she said, still looking around for Spirit. "Good heavens! Are you early?"

"Where's Spirit?" I yelled at her.

"Here's around here. He'll be right back. He just went for a little run."

"You lost him! You lost him, didn't you?"

"No, honey, he's not lost. He saw a fox and ran after it. But he'll be back. He does this all the time; it's not a big deal."

"You let him out here without a leash all the time? What's wrong with you? I knew this would happen! I knew he'd run away!" My accusations flew at her without restraint.

"Lily stop this!" she demanded as I searched the field for my dog. "He's fine; I promise you."

"How can you promise me anything? You're a liar! You lie about everything! Why should I believe you?" I ran toward the lake and away from my mother, who stood helplessly in the field.

"Lily! What are you talking about?" She whistled for the dog as I continued to run toward the lake. "Argh!" she cried out. "Lily! Please! You don't need to panic!" she called after me.

But her words were muffled by the sound of my heart beating and the rush of wind swirling in my head as I ran as fast as I could away from her.

"Lily!"

I climbed through the split-rail fence and glanced over my shoulder to catch sight of her running with Spirit close behind. Then came the sound of screeching tires and a blaring car horn.

"Oh, dear God!" she cried.

Then someone yelled, "Call 911!"

CHAPTER 12

FROM TOMB TO WOMB

"Call 911!" Those were the last words I heard on the day I decided to leave myself behind. I still sensed the desperation and fear all around me. How was I supposed to tune it out? I mean, it felt like I was being crushed by everyone else's emotions. Take the guy who hit me, for example. He was giving off a *terrible* vibe. His heavy footsteps shook the ground where I was lying as he paced back and forth, back and forth. I didn't blame him; he had a good reason to be upset. Even if it wasn't his fault. I wanted to tell him that. But I didn't.

The worst part was my mother. You can imagine how she felt, right? Well…she clung to me so tightly that she nearly squeezed every breath of life out of me. Her face was buried in my chest, and my shirt was soaked from her slobber and tears. Spirit was there too, licking my face and adding to my dampness. He almost made me smile. But I fought as hard as I could and overcame the urge to open my eyes.

"They'll be fine," I told myself. "They have each other. They don't need me. Not now. Not like this."

It was the hardest thing I ever had to do, but I knew this was how it had to be. If I went back now, nothing would change. My life would be more out of control than ever because my fears would totally consume me. And being so close to losing me would make my mother more protective than ever. She might even start lying all the time just so I wouldn't go off the deep end. I would never be able to trust her again. I hated what this was doing to her, and I wished with all my heart that there was another way. But I had to see this through, or I couldn't go back at all.

In some weird way, the accident was a blessing. It was as if someone handed me a golden opportunity to escape the chaos and confusion of my life and slip away for a while to regroup. To catch my breath. I don't know. It's not that I wanted to die. I just wanted to start over. To go all the way back...inside my mother's womb...and be born again. This time...I wanted my father to be there when I arrived.

The instant after being struck, I tucked myself into a fetal position and cannonballed into a pool of swirling dark water, where I bobbed up and down and all around until I settled into a peaceful cradle of liquid love. I felt completely safe inside my bubble of bliss, and I floated selfishly in the overwhelming serenity I had immersed myself in. Then, I drowned the awareness of my mother's pain and decided I would never leave this place. This thought echoed with the sound of my beating heart, and I was instantly aware of, yet completely unaffected by, the knowledge that I was still alive.

I might have remained in that tranquil state forever had it not been for the turbulence created by my mother's suffering. Her desperate sobs convulsed into a tsunami of sorrow that crashed over me with such ferocity, I thought for a moment that I might be consumed by her agony. I nearly gave up. I didn't know what to do. I couldn't go back. I couldn't stay where I was. So I closed my eyes and pushed against her with all my strength. I pushed and pushed until with one mighty, determined shove, I separated myself from my mother's will. And landed...headfirst...in a lush green meadow of thick, velvety grass.

PART II
U-R-HERE

CHAPTER 13

BORN AGAIN

My head was spinning much too fast to be lifted, so I kept my eyes closed and lay perfectly still until the swirling subsided. I was acutely aware that everything around and about me was different, yet I was not at all anxious about where I was or what was happening. Enveloped in the peace of an indescribable love, my heart overflowed with the promise of new life. All my doubts and fears had vanished, and in their place, was the absolute assurance that nothing would ever come against me. I knew I was not alone. I was in the presence of my father.

"I am always within," I heard a voice say from somewhere near my heart, "and you are never without."

"Without what?" I wondered as a delightful wisp of honeysuckle danced beneath my nose. "Oh my," I said, distracted by the fragrance, "I must be near the woods."

But the image I had of the woods near the cottage in Lindenwood instantly burst like a bubble as my eyes were awakened to the brilliant abundance that existed all around me. Nothing I had ever experienced in my days on earth could have prepared me for the wonder that assaulted my senses and stirred the very fiber of my being. My sight held me spellbound by an infinite spectrum of colors that pulsated through every blade, blossom, and leaf as they danced to the rhythm of the silent, gentle wind.

I was aware of my presence in this measure of time, and I sensed that I was but a single note in an eternal symphony that was created long before the world began. I was mindful that my every movement altered the frequencies of all that was around me, so I moved slowly and deliberately until I was in a seated position. The succulent, sweet scent of honeysuckle twirled around my nose once again and beckoned me to follow its vaporous trail. I smiled at its urging and gazed into the distance at the playful vine as it wound itself around the trunk of a tall oak tree and moved with ease toward the branches above.

"My word!" I declared. "You certainly know how to climb." I laughed as the honeysuckle clung to the trunk of the tree that welcomed it so graciously. "It's as if the oak had been waiting for the vine all along...so he could be complete." The thought of being made whole by the presence of another overwhelmed me, and a tear slid down my cheek as I looked to the heavens and gave thanks to the One Who Provides.

"Wait a minute," I said, snapping out of my grateful state. "That doesn't sound like me." I sprung to my feet and began a careful examination of all that I could see of who I was. I stretched out my arms and noted the light-brown corduroy sleeves with soft, pink plaid lining that were rolled up just beneath my elbows. The jacket, which seemed rather small, hung over a short green shirt that was dotted with rosebuds and finished with white scalloped trim.

"These aren't my clothes," I muttered, looking down at the multipocketed khaki pants and gray rubber boots. Pulling a handful of wavy, auburn hair over my shoulder, I exclaimed, "And this is *not* my hair!"

I twisted and twirled in every direction, looking up and down, over and under, inside and out before I decided I was no longer in Lindenwood. To my great surprise, I wasn't unhappy about this revelation. In fact, I was excited.

I scanned the landscape and listened intently for clues as to where I might be. A cool breeze washed over me, and with it came the sweet smell of dry earth after a long-awaited rain.

"Water!" I said, as the sound of a babbling brook trickled into my ears. I quickly followed it down a hill and through a cluster of trees to a pool of crystal-clear water. The water seemed unconcerned with the obstacles that were in its path as it rippled over rocks and floated around branches, making its way toward a destination that was completely unknown.

"The water certainly has great faith about where it's going," I said as a piece of bark swerved around a large rock and was followed by some leaves and twigs that were all riding the current. "And it looks like there are others who want to go there, too! Have a wonderful journey!" I called out as I waved to those who were on their way to somewhere else.

Glancing at the small hand that was waving in the air, I wondered who was attached to the other end. I scanned the stream for still water and ran down the bank to a patch of soft, mossy earth. I knelt down and planted my hands as close to the water as possible and leaned as far forward as my balance would allow. Peering into the crystalline pool beneath me, I saw…nothing.

"That's impossible," I said, staring into the dark water.

I glanced up at the branches of the trees that stretched above my head and the clouds that floated in the azure sky. But the water reflected none of the beauty that existed all around it, including that of the face gazing on it now.

"Oh, my heavens!" I declared to the unrelenting pool. "It's true!" I leaned over the water to search for my reflection once again, but it was not there. "And…I'm her," I said, confirming what I already knew. "I'm Mira."

The words had no sooner left my lips when a voice rang out from the top of the hill on two lilting notes—one high, one low.

"Meeer-ahhh! Diii-nahhh!"

And my now small voice sang back its sweet reply, "'Kaaay, Mahhhm!"

CHAPTER 14

U-R-HERE, BUT
WHO ARE YOU?

I came upon a tiny thatched hut near the stream as I walked up the hill toward the house, and taking just a moment, I wandered over and looked inside. "Hello!" I called out. "Is anyone home?" I didn't expect an answer, although I was hoping for a sign that the bunny hut was occupied. "Well," I rationalized, excusing the inhabitants for being elsewhere, "it is quite a lovely day. It's understandable that you've chosen to be outdoors. I suspect you'll return when the sun sets. I do hope you have a very pleasant evening. Good night!"

The windows of the cottage were open, and the smell of something wonderful cooking in the kitchen wafted through the air. "I hope its Love You Stew," I said to the self that was inside me, for I no longer felt like Lily, but I didn't feel fully like Mira either.

"What if they know I'm not Mira?" I wondered as I stepped onto the porch. But the thought left my mind as quickly as it appeared when I turned the knob and burst happily through the kitchen door.

"Mmm! Something smells yummy! What are you cooking, Grammy?"

"Why, I believe that yummy smell is Love You Stew! But it's not for little girls with mud all over them."

I looked down at my knees, which were caked with mud from kneeling next to the stream. "Oops, I'm sorry, Grammy!" I stepped outside and brushed the mud and moss from my pants, took off my boots, and went back inside. "How's this?" I asked.

I stood by the door, waiting for her approval before venturing any farther. The room was just as I had imagined it, with lots of cabinets and plenty of counter space for rolling dough and preparing large meals. Grammy stood in front of a white cast-iron stove, stirring the pot of stew with one hand while opening one of the oven doors with the other.

She turned her head my way and smiled. "Much better, dear! Why don't you run upstairs and take a bath before dinner? I suspect there'll be a few guests joining us this evening, and I could use your help to get things ready."

"Okay, Gram," I said happily. "Where's Mum?"

"She's getting a few jars of figs and nuts from the cellar. I want to make a lemon millet fig cake for dessert. Mr. Wallace will be with us tonight, and he's very fond of fig cake."

"Mmm, I'm very fond of it too!"

Grammy laughed as I ran down the hall.

"The stairs are to my right," I thought correctly. "Five steps, then a landing. Another right turn, then seven steps to the hallway."

When I reached the top of the stairs, I instinctively turned left and walked confidently into the main bathroom at the end of the hall. The big white tub with clawed feet was where I expected it to be. A stopper hung from a chain attached to the faucet, which I fit it into the drain, then turned the water on full blast. Freshly laundered towels were neatly stacked in the closet, and I buried my face in one to get a whiff of the sweet summer scent before placing it on the rack by the tub. I took off my clothes, placed them in the hamper, and stuck my big toe in to test the water. The temperature was just right, and the water was deep and inviting, so I took a big breath, pinched my nose, and slipped as far down as I could go. My long, wavy hair floated wispily around me, and I swished my head from side to side to keep it from sinking.

I was completely content underwater, and I might have stayed there all evening if Mum hadn't come in to check on me. I felt her presence as she entered, but I was too preoccupied with being fully submerged to react. With my eyes shut tight and nose still pinched, I tilted my head back to let my thick, wet mane drift lazily behind me. Then I lifted my face above the water just far enough to take a gulp of air, and I slipped back to the bottom once again. Mum knelt beside the tub, her arms resting on the rim.

"Mira," she chortled happily as she leaned over the water.

My heart leapt at the sound of her voice, and my head popped out of the water like a balloon that was suddenly released from the bottom of a pool. I spat and sputtered while trying to part the heavy, wet curls from my face. She reached for a towel and gently dried the droplets that clung to my lashes, freeing my eyes to gaze upon her beautiful face. I was instantly in love with her. Her crystal-blue eyes were as bright as the stars on a cloudless night, and her smile seemed to tickle her cheeks, which somehow made her eyes shine even brighter. It seemed as though every good and perfect thing that existed in this world or any other was alive within her, and I smiled at her with my whole heart.

I couldn't take my eyes from her as she chatted about the garden she and Grammy were planning while she shampooed my hair and washed the bottoms of my feet. I listened intently and occasionally added an "Ooh!" or "Ahh!" to let her know I was interested. But I didn't want to interrupt a single word, as her voice was like a lovely instrument, and every sound was music to my ears.

When the shampooing was done, she pulled the stopper from the drain and turned the water on, so I could stick my head under the faucet and rinse out all the soap. It took a while, and the tub was nearly empty when she placed a plastic bowl under the stream of water, filled it to the brim, and poured it over me from my neck down. It was nice and warm. When she was satisfied that I was free from any soapy residue, she took my hands and helped me out of the empty tub and wrapped a sweet-smelling towel around me.

"Dry off, darling, and brush your hair," she said as she kissed my forehead. "I'm going to help Grammy in the kitchen. We'll see you soon."

"Okay, Mum," I said without missing a beat, and I gazed at her in awe until she disappeared through the door.

Water trickled from my hair and down my spine as I stood transfixed, staring at the closed door. I swallowed hard as my eyes welled with tears. "She believes I am Mira," I said to myself. And I believed it too.

I wrapped the towel around me and winced as I reached for a hairbrush that sat on a small table beneath the window. I was expecting this to be an arduous task; but to my surprise, the brush glided through my thick, wavy locks without so much as a snag. "Everything about her is perfect," I thought. And suddenly the idea of leaving my old, highly imperfect self behind seemed like a stroke of sheer genius.

A small tube of toothpaste and a soft-bristled brush sat in a blue plastic cup that was settled in the well of a wall-mounted holder near the sink. After a vigorous brushing, a good rinse, and a spit, I wiped my mouth with the hand towel and stared at the cabinet above the basin. I couldn't quite put my finger on it, but something about the cabinet bothered me.

The door was nearly flush to the wall, so the cabinet must have been built into it. But why wasn't there a knob to open it? I tilted my head to the side and leaned over the sink to look under the cabinet for a groove that would aid in opening the door. But there was none. I tucked my fingers under the frame and was about to give it a tug when I was acutely aware that I was about to break a long-standing house rule.

"Don't go looking for trouble," I heard a voice say.

"Thank you," I replied, without a thought as to whom I was speaking. "That's very good advice!"

I hurried down the hall toward my bedroom. I was already getting excited about seeing Mum and Grammy, and I couldn't wait to get dressed and join them in the kitchen. I turned the knob, flung open my bedroom door, and stepped onto a white furry carpet that felt like a cloud of spun silk. I wiggled my toes into the dense pile until they had nearly disappeared. The sensation was unlike anything I'd ever experienced, yet it was delightfully familiar. "This house was built for falling in love with everything in it… over and over again."

"Love and care for all things," a voice reminded me. "And for all things, give thanks to the One Who Provides."

"That's the key," I said aloud as I danced through my room on a silky cloud.

CHAPTER 15

MEETING DADDY

There was much milling about in the kitchen as the visitors flowed steadily in. It was then that I first witnessed the miracle of provision, as a bounty of food appeared from nowhere and the house expanded to ensure everyone was comfortable. The table, which was perfect for four earlier in the day, seated twenty or more by the time dinner was served.

Grammy smiled as she handed bowls and platters of fresh vegetables, grains, chicken, and fish to those who offered a helping hand. Mum was making a big pitcher of lemonade when I walked into the room. She turned to greet me, as did everyone else.

"Hello, Mira dear! You look lovely today!"

"Mira! So happy to see you!"

"Hello, everyone!" I said as I made a beeline to Grammy and Mum. "I'm so happy you're all here."

Mum leaned over and kissed my forehead as she handed me a pile of napkins and flatware. I was just about to start setting the table when a pair of hands covered my eyes, and a deep, round voice said, "Guess who, or you shan't move!"

I heard Mum giggle, and Grammy said, "Oh Jairus! You can't fool her. That child of yours would know your touch anywhere."

Child of yours. The words swirled around in my brain, and my heart skipped a beat when I realized that the hands that were touching my face belonged to my father.

"Daddy!" I squealed in unbridled joy as the rest of the house fell silent.

My eyes were weepy when he spun me around and lifted me to kiss my cheek. I wrapped my arms around his neck so tight that I nearly strangled him. But I couldn't help myself. This was my father. My daddy! I'd waited so long to meet him, and now I was holding him. And he was holding me.

"Good heavens," he said, loosening my grip. "I haven't gotten a greeting like that in a month of Sundays." He lowered me to the ground and stroked the top of my head with his gentle hands. "I can't think of a better way to get a hello from my little girl."

I stood motionless, with my eyes wide and a big, sappy grin on my face. "Daddy!" I sighed.

He laughed and pinched my cheeks. "Yes, my darling, I am most definitely your daddy. And I love every moment of it. Now, what do you say we help Mum set the table? You already have a handful of napkins and flatware. I'll grab some dishes, and we'll get this show on the road."

He pulled a stack of dinner plates from the cabinet and said, "Follow me! We will start a parade."

Several folks had been watching us and decided to join in the fun. Some picked up more dishes, others grabbed cups and saucers, and they fell in line behind the grand marshal.

"Ha-ha! We've done it, Mira! Look at the splendid parade we've made."

"Woo-hoo!" I giggled as I raised my hand filled with forks like a baton.

I followed the leader down the hall, through the living room, onto the porch, and back into the dining area, where we each put down our items and collectively created the most beautifully set table in the happiest house that ever was.

Then my father stood back to look at this masterpiece and said, "All glory and honor to the One Who Is, Was, and Always Will Be."

And everyone responded with a resounding "Amen!"

CHAPTER 16

MEETING MICAH

There were many seats at the expanded table, but only one was empty. It was clear that the empty chair was intentional, as no one tried to sit in it even though there was a place setting in front of it. I was quite curious about the vacant seat when another visitor wandered in.

"Micah! We're so happy you could join us," Mum said as she stood to greet him. "Please take your usual seat. You've come at the perfect time. We were just about to say grace."

"Thank you, Mum," he said as he kissed her cheek. I apologize for being late. But I was fishing with the boys on the lake today when out of the blue, Peter decided to get out of the boat...without me!"

"Good heavens!" Grammy cried, as everyone gasped. "What happened?"

"Ha-ha!" He laughed as he made a loud clap with his hands. "He sunk like a rock, of course."

The room filled with laughter as Micah looked at me from the other end of the table and smiled.

Who is he? I wondered as I smiled back. He was not like anyone I'd ever seen. His long, dark hair and short beard suited him but clearly set him apart from the other clean-shaven men at the table. He was tall and lean with piercing blue eyes and a smile that ended in a deep dimple on just one side of his face. He wore sandals, jeans, and a white collarless shirt with rolled-up sleeves that looked like it had just been taken from the dryer. But it wasn't his appearance that set him apart from everyone else in the room. It was the warm glow that lit up his face that pulled you in, and I wanted to get close to him just to experience his light.

The room quieted and then fell silent as we reached for the hands next to us and bowed our heads to pray. Daddy gave thanks to the One Who Provides for the gifts of family, friends, and the beautiful meal set before us. "And thank You for sending the One Who Sits at Your Right Hand. His presence is a blessing to us all."

Just before the amen, Micah added, "And if it is Your will, Father, would you please see to it that Peter dries out quickly this time?"

The room filled with laughter, and the chatter began. It was a magical evening that was unlike anything I'd ever imagined, and I was captivated by the outpouring of love and friendship in the room. The abundance of food quickly dwindled to a few bits, and every delicious bite was followed by a sigh of sheer delight from one or more very satisfied guest. Mum excused me from the table when Micah asked if we could take a walk to the stream. I was happy to go for a walk, but I was so full, I was afraid I might roll down the hill.

"Could you please save some leftovers for the animals?" I asked as I stood from the table, although the promise of leftovers seemed unlikely.

"We saved a small plate in the fridge," Grammy said as she gave me a wink, and I skipped happily out the door after Micah.

The evening air was cool as the sun had begun to set, casting tones of pink, yellow, and gray against the soft-blue sky. As we walked through the thick, green meadow, the earth seemed to come alive under our feet. The branches of the giant elms bent down as we passed, and Micah smiled.

"They're magnificent, don't you think?"

I was in awe of the way nature was responding to his presence and I nodded, as I was unable to speak. Birds were singing, crickets were chirping, and I heard the brook babbling even though we were still high on the hill.

"It's you! You're doing this, aren't you?"

"Yes. I'm doing it. But so are you. The earth responds to those who love and respect her. She is greeting us as her friends because she trusts us."

"But this has never happened before. I've been outside every day since I was born, and the branches never bowed to me."

Micah laughed. "They bow to you every time they see you. You just never noticed." He stooped down next to a bed of English ivy, and I watched the vines stretch toward him.

"Come over here," he said, and I took one small step closer to him, not wanting to disturb his encounter with the vine. He laughed. "Come on, silly girl! You've done this a million times. I just want to show you what you've missed."

The thick grass tickled my bare ankles as I sat cross-legged next to Micah. Leaning toward the bed of ivy, I invited it to come to me. And…it did! Micah's face beamed, and so did mine. I reached my hand toward the vines, and they slowly wound around my fingers. I let out a little gasp, but I was afraid to move, for fear they would leave.

"It's okay," Micah said. "Just relax. Talk to them as you always do."

I took a deep breath and let myself be what was inside of me.

"Good evening, lovely ivy. You've made me so happy, I'm at a loss for words. To think that you've been waiting all this time for me to truly see you. Thank you! I promise…I'll never not see you again."

Micah stood up and gently placed the ivy back on the ground. "Let's meander on," he said. "There's bound to be a few friends waiting down the hill."

"I'll see you in the morning, dear ivy. And I'll dream of your tender hugs tonight." Lowering my hand to the ground, the vines unwound from my fingers and slipped back into the thick patch. I sat motionless for a moment, still amazed by what I'd just witnessed. I turned to look at Micah, who was smiling down on me.

"That was the most amazing thing that's ever happened to me. How did you know?"

Micah's smile grew wider, and his brilliant eyes sparkled in the dimming light of day. "It's a truth taught to me by my Father about loving each other the way we are loved by Him. It applies to all living things. You love nature so well, it is only natural for you to be loved in return."

"Your father must be very smart!"

"He is very wise!" Micah reached out his hand to help me up, and we strolled down the hill toward the stream. It was dusky, and many of the flowers had closed their petals for the coming night. But as we approached, they began opening into full bloom. First the crocus. Then the poppies. The big, red-and-white hibiscus were the most magnificent. Their wide, papery petals stretched out to greet us and then opened to their full glory. I cupped my hands over my mouth in awe of their beauty, and once again tears of joy stung my eyes.

Micah nudged me. "It's unusual for you to be in the garden at dusk, and they're very happy to see you. Say hello and thank them for their beautiful offering."

"Oh, glorious ones! You honor me with your presence. I am truly grateful for each and every one of you. Thank you so very much for coming out to greet us."

I blew a kiss into the garden, and a single tear fell into the center of a daylily. The open bloom folded its petals as if drinking my tear. It swayed back and forth with graceful fluidity, then burst open once again with its face stretched toward me. I gasped at the wonder of it all as Micah laughed and danced behind me. He grabbed my hands and spun me around as we praised the One Who Provides for His gift of life to all things.

It was getting dark, and we could see that most of the guests were leaving, although a few were still milling about in the kitchen with Mum and Grammy.

"Perhaps we should leave our walk to the stream for another day," Micah suggested. "Let's be good guests and see if there's anything left for us to do."

I nodded with a smile. I was still overwhelmed by all that had transpired in our short journey and I was not at all certain that my heart could hold another surprise. We turned toward the house and headed slowly up the hill, stepping gently and quietly through the long grass so as not to disturb those who were sleeping. The light that remained of day drifted down through the branches and leaves of the trees, casting shadows that were foggy and gray. Micah began to say something about light and darkness when something caught my eye in the wooded area beyond the house.

"Micah! Did you see that?"

"See what? What was it?"

"I don't know. Something in the woods." The figure moved again behind the trees. "There! Did you see it that time? It looks like a person. Who could it be? Are they watching us?"

Micah wasn't startled by the shadowy figure, and I was not afraid. I sensed it was in need of something but lacked the courage to come out of the darkness.

"Ah! That is a Seeker," he said. "Seekers search for something they cannot find because they look in all the wrong places."

"What are they searching for?"

"Truth."

"The woods seem like a strange place to search for truth."

Micah nodded.

"But where will they find it?" I asked.

"In the Word, little one. Truth is found in the Word. But they are too afraid to let go of the *world*, so they search everywhere but where it is. Some never find it. They get as far as the universe or themselves, but the answers can't be found in the stars or in us. They are found in the One Who Provides. And in His Word."

"The secret to a happy life," I whispered.

"That's right, dear heart." He smiled and put his hand on my shoulder. "Grammy has taught you well."

We reached the house when all the dishes had been cleared and put away. The table had shrunk once again to accommodate four, and the last visitors waved good-bye as they walked out the door.

"Well, it looks like our walk was perfectly timed," Micah joked.

"That's right, son. You've managed to escape doing dishes again." Father laughed as Mum and Grammy dried their hands and removed their aprons.

"We can't thank you enough for coming, Micah. Your presence is always a blessing but very much appreciated at this time."

Micah took Mum and Grammy's hands and held them in his as he stood in front of the Two. He kissed the tips of their fingers and blessed them as he thanked them for their hospitality and faith. Then he put his arm around Daddy's shoulder and told him he was doing a good work in our home and his rewards would be many. The two men hugged, and my father's eye held a tear. Micah was clearly special and very much loved. He turned to me and reached for my hands.

"And you, young lady, have some truly remarkable gifts! Thank you for the delightful stroll. It's always a great joy being with you. Let's do it again soon."

I was overjoyed, and I couldn't wait to see him again. "Oh yes! Please! Thank you, Micah. That was the most wonderful walk I've ever had."

Everyone smiled down on me, and the warmth of their love was overwhelming. Micah kissed the top of my head and walked toward the door.

"Sleep in peace, dear ones. I will see you soon."

We stood together watching as he walked down the path and then suddenly disappeared into the night.

"Whoa! Where did he go?" I asked.

"He knows the Way." Daddy sighed as he gazed into the darkness. "I'm sure he'll show it to you one day soon."

I was curious as to what he meant, but before I could ask him, Mum took my hand. "Mira darling," she began, "it's getting late. Run upstairs and get ready for bed. I'll be up in a minute to tuck you in."

Grammy and Daddy kissed me good-night, and I hurried up the steps. I had no sooner finished brushing my teeth and hair and putting on my pajamas when Mum appeared at my bedroom door. When I climbed into bed, she pulled the covers around me and then sat down next to me.

"So…it sounds like you and Micah had a very nice time together."

"Oh yes, Mum! He's the most amazing person I've ever known. He loves the trees and flowers and animals as much as I do. And they love him."

Mum smiled. "He showed you a gift that you hadn't seen before, right?"

"Yes! As we walked through the garden, the elms lowered their branches, and the flowers opened their petals in full bloom. And a tendril of ivy stretched toward me and wound itself around my finger."

Mum's eyes glistened.

"We've witnessed that many times when you were among those you dearly love. But if we had told you about it, you might not have fully understood. Micah knew you had to see it for yourself. I am so happy to know you are in tune to this very special part of you. All praise and glory to the One Who Provides."

"Amen!" I declared with a huge smile on my face.

Mum smiled back.

"Amen!" she echoed and kissed my forehead. "Good night, my darling. Sleep well. Tomorrow waits just for you."

CHAPTER 17

WHATEVER IS RIGHT, WHATEVER IS PURE

A single chirp was heard outside my window, calling me into the day. I bolted out of bed and thrust open the curtains to let in the dim morning light. It was still very early, and the world was soaking in the dew. I got dressed in record time and ran down the stairs, following the delicious aroma into the kitchen.

"Grammy!" I called out before entering the room. "Something smells sooo good!"

The beautiful old woman stood by the chopping block, surrounded by mixing bowls, spoons, and batters. Her long-braided hair looked like spun silver that laid down her back, nearly reaching her waist. She turned at the sound of my voice and greeted me with a big smile and her warm brown eyes.

"Good morning, darling! You're up nice and early today."

"Oh yes, Grammy! A bird was chirping in the tree out-side my window, and I'm sure he was inviting me out to play."

Grammy laughed. The large book that was always by her side sat open amid the kitchen tools and ingredients.

"What does the Word have to say this morning, Gram? Is there a recipe for the day ahead?

"Oh my, yes! The Word is a recipe-for-life book! I'll tell you what," she said as she brushed some flour from her hands and took off her apron, "the cobbler won't be done for some time. Why don't we sit on the porch for a bit, and I'll share what I'm reading with you?"

"That would be wonderful," I said excitedly, as I'd been looking forward to spending more time with her. I slipped on my shoes and held the door for Grammy as she hugged her favorite recipe book close to her heart.

"Thank you, dear," she said. "Your manners are highly polished today!"

Compliments from Grammy were treasures that I want-ed to collect and store in my heart forever. Every one of them sparkled like a diamond but was more valuable than the most precious stone. She was always sincere and mind-ful of what she spoke, for she knew that words are powerful.

"A gentle answer turns away wrath," Grammy once said, "but a harsh word stirs up anger."

I thought that was very wise, and I told her so.

"Wise words, indeed! But not my own. They are writ-ten in the book of Proverbs, chapter 15, verse 1. They were penned by the wisest man who ever lived." Her face was aglow as she spoke about the Word. "It is the only book we'll ever need, you know, for the secrets to a full and happy life can be found within its pages. If we spend time in the Word and in prayer every day, we will be immeasurably blessed, for we will come to know the book's Author."

And something in my heart said that she was right.

We sat side by side on the porch swing and looked through the yard that led to the stream. From where we sat, I could see that the leftovers I'd placed under the tree were gone, and it made me happy to know that a few woodland friends had full bellies this morning.

"I wish I could feed all the creatures in U-R-Here," I said as we rocked gently on the swing. Grammy's bright eyes twinkled as she pulled me close to her.

"There is a plan in place for all living things," she reminded me. "But I'm quite sure the ones who live in our meadow and woods are very grateful that you remember them each night."

"And I'm grateful for them, too," I said earnestly.

I felt safe snuggled next to Grammy and perfectly content. Her soft, cotton blouse smelled like lemon snap cookies that were fresh from the oven, and my mouth watered just thinking of the delicious treats that awaited me.

Grammy placed the open book on her lap.

"The Word spoke to me this morning about our hearts," she said. "It says that we are to watch over them with all diligence, for from them flow the springs of life."

"What does that mean, Gram? What are the springs of life?"

"The springs of life are living waters that hold promises of hope and prosperity for those who love Him and follow His Word. Knowing how He sees us keeps us on a steady path toward our destinies and His purpose for creating us.

But when we do not know who we are in His eyes, we are like twigs that float aimlessly through the current of life without direction. And we must beware, for we can be easily led astray by those whose perception of us is not in line with the Creator's. They can set us on a path that we were never intended to travel, and we miss great blessings that He had for us along the way."

"How does He see our hearts, Grammy?"

"He sees our hearts as He created them: whole, pure, filled with compassion, patience, kindness, joy and love. The world will tempt us every day, and the Enemy will deceive us with lies and accusations. But if we remember that we have been given a spirit of peace, faith, and love, we will overcome temptation, fear, anger, and sin. And the very best time to start protecting these heavenly qualities is when we're young—before we become jaded by the world and fooled by the devil."

Grammy turned the pages of the Word to Philippians 4:8 and read the verse aloud:

Finally, brothers and sisters, whatever is true, whatever is noble, whatever is right, whatever is pure, whatever is lovely, whatever is admirable – if anything is excellent or praiseworthy – think about such things.

"That's beautiful, Grammy!" I lifted my head up to find her smile. "I want to do that every day," I decided. "It seems like there's always something we can complain about. But why focus on things that are wrong when there's so much that's right to dwell on?"

Grammy didn't answer, but she gave me a hug, and I sensed that there was a deeper truth waiting to be discovered. I sat in silence and turned my attention to the words she'd read, but the harder I looked for revelation, the farther away it got from me. I was exasperated.

"You're relying on your own abilities to get you where you want to go," Grammy said, as if reading my mind. "You must let go and let Him take you where He already has you. The journey is easy when we shed the burden of *self* and trust the One who knew us long before we were born."

But, how was I to put my *self* aside and follow Him? I was more than willing! I just didn't know how. It was puzzling, to say the least. Soon, I found myself trying very hard to figure it out, and once again I was moving further and further away from where I wanted to be.

Grammy kissed the top of my head and put my hand in hers.

"Who would you say is the most miraculous person you know?"

I was about to say "Daddy" when Micah's face appeared before me. He was, by far, the most remarkable and, yes, the most miraculous person I'd ever met. He was all the things the passage spoke of and so much more. As I thought about him, I began to experience a lightness about me. It started in my belly and then spread to my chest and shoulders. It moved swiftly and purposefully, and when it was done, I was filled with so much lightness that my *self* just floated away. And in its place was the overwhelming peace that comes when your life is in the hands of the One who knew you before you were born.

I read the passage from Philippians that lay open on Grammy's lap, and the voice that was somewhere near my heart said, "Be such things."

"Be such things," I whispered.

It was in a single moment that it all came together. The voice somewhere near my heart began to speak through my mouth. I knew right away that the words and the wisdom they carried did not come from me. I also knew they were absolutely true. Grammy knew it, too.

"We are called to *be,*" the voice began, "created to *be*. It's about *being* the things that the Word says we should think about every day. Because, if we *are* pure, if we *are* lovely, and if we *are* admirable in the things we do and say…then we will be an example for others to follow. We can *be* the excellent or praiseworthy thing that others will think about. We can *be* a light in the darkness that will help people who have lost their way."

The swing slowed until it was nearly still as Grammy and I silently pondered the words I'd just spoken. A power that was far greater than anything I'd ever known filled me with a love that surpassed a world driven by feelings and emotions. This was a divine love—a love that didn't seek approval or acceptance from the world but sought instead salvation and truth for all humankind. It felt completely selfless and inconceivably powerful. And the power moved within me like an electric current that set off a flow of charges throughout my body. It wasn't uncomfortable… but it was startling. It made me tremble. Grammy pulled me closer to her, and the surge passed through her and back to me. I felt a warm glow being shared between us that was both brilliant and peaceful.

"When we love as He intended," Grammy explained, "He sends the Spirit to live with us and in us. The power you are experiencing is the Spirit that is in you. He will help you and guide you through all the days of your life, so you will never be alone. It is a miraculous gift from the One who created you and knows your heart, dear. All praise and glory to His name."

A gentle breeze blew through the leaves of the giant oak. I remained content, wrapped up in Grammy's arms, nurtured by His love. I wanted to stay in that place forever, but the day ahead beckoned us to come.

"I think I'd better check on the cobbler," she said, heeding the call of the day. "Why don't you take a nice walk by the stream to see if anyone is awake?"

"That's a lovely idea, Grammy." I sat up and turned to look deeply in her eyes, as I was certain that I would see her soul in them. "Thank you for your wisdom and for sharing the Word with me, Gram. I feel brand new today, and it's an amazing feeling…as if…I can do anything."

Grammy leaned down and kissed my cheek. "He adores you, darling. You are His precious daughter. And it is a great privilege to see what He's doing in you. You are going to make great contributions to this world, dear. Many will be blessed by your beautiful heart."

She smiled and kissed my cheek. Then she walked toward the kitchen door with the Word pressed to her heart.

CHAPTER 18

THE FINDER OF SEEKERS

"Perhaps the rabbits are having breakfast," I thought as I headed down the hill toward the hut. "We must be very quiet," I reminded myself as I got closer. "We don't want to startle them so early in the morning!" As I tiptoed down the hill, I heard something rustling in the underbrush. I stood perfectly still. But the noise stopped. I took a few more steps and then...there it was again. I stayed frozen in place, trying hard to hear where the sound was coming from.

"Whoever it is, they're very close by." I squatted in front of the dense brush in hopes of catching a glimpse of who was inside. Suddenly a rabbit leapt from the bush and nearly landed on my lap.

"Whoop!" I yelled and tumbled backward onto the grass. "Who startled whom?" I giggled as I lay gazing up at the clouds that floated slowly in the morning sky. Something in my peripheral vision caught my attention, but I chose not to move for fear of scaring it away. Keeping my eye on the image that had not yet come into full view, I remained quiet and perfectly still until at last I saw him. His long ears stood straight up as he sat on his back haunches, studying me. I dared not move a muscle as he crept slowly toward me with his head low to the ground.

"Be still," I heard a voice say, "and he will come to you."

My excitement grew as I watched him move cautiously toward me. He was grayish-brown with dark, glassy eyes that were fixed on me. He sat up as he got closer; I never flinched. His nose and whiskers twitched wildly as he sat within an arm's reach from me, his soft white underbelly exposed.

"Oh, my heavens!" I declared to myself. This was so amazing. Slowly, the rabbit crept beside me. My heart raced as he crouched next to me, sniffing all around. I smiled, although I tried hard not to, fearing he might run away. Instead he stepped onto my belly just above my folded hands and curled up in that space as if it were a comfortable chair. He was only there for a moment when he looked into my eyes, wiggled his long ears, and hopped away. I was spellbound, unable to believe what my eyes had just witnessed. What my body had just felt. I sensed the presence of Micah and looked around for a sign of him.

"Oh Micah! Did you see that? Did you see how he came to me?"

I heard his playful laugh as clearly as if he were standing beside me, and I couldn't wait to share my incredible experience with him. I jumped to my feet and ran up the hill as fast as I could. I was nearly at the house when I heard a strange sound coming from the woods. I stood perfectly still and listened. Sunlight trickled through the branches of the trees that were heavy with darkness just hours ago. The figure that was no more than a shadow in the night began to take form in the light of day. I walked quickly toward it in hopes that I might be able to direct it to the Truth. But the figure was too busy searching to notice me. The futility of its actions filled me with sorrow, as I was helpless in its plight. It knelt down and brushed away pine needles and twigs from the ground but uncovered nothing.

"You won't find what you're looking for there," I said, loud enough to be heard. But the figure paid no attention and wandered aimlessly into the woods. "Please! Wait!" I called out. "I can help you!" But it was gone. A heavy burden was suddenly placed upon my heart as I walked toward the house, where Mum and Grammy were busy preparing our morning meal.

"There's my darling daughter," Mum said happily.

But I was too preoccupied with the Seeker to respond, and I walked mindlessly through the kitchen and to my room. I sat on the window seat and gazed at the woods where the Seeker had been. My heart was troubled. I thought about how lonely and sad it must be to wander every day. Mum soon appeared at the door, drying her hands on a dish towel. She sat facing me on the cushioned sill and patiently waited for me to speak.

"Mum," I began, without glancing her way, "do you know about the seekers?"

"Yes, dear. Why do you ask?"

"Because there's one living in our woods. I think it searches day and night." I turned my face to hers. "Micah says they're searching for the Truth, but they can't find it where they're looking."

"That's right," she said. "Many fall short of finding it because they believed the lie that the key to happiness can be found within themselves, when, in fact, true happiness comes when we let go of *self* and follow Him."

I looked back to the woods. "It must be very frightening to live in darkness all the time."

"I'm sure it is. That's why we must take every opportunity we have to show people where true love can be found. It all begins with the Word. It's the very best weapon we have against the lies of the Enemy, who tells us we're not good enough, smart enough, rich enough, or beautiful enough for the One to love us. What is true is that He never leaves us or forsakes us, no matter how far we stray from him."

"Do you think the Seeker in our woods strayed from Him?"

"I believe she thinks He strayed from her."

"The Seeker is a woman?" My heart broke into a million pieces, and I was filled with a desire to know everything about her.

"Yes, dear. She's been with us for a very long time. Since she was a young girl. She left for a while, and we hoped she had found the Way. But we now know that she stopped seeking because she stopped believing. Seeing her again gives us great hope, although we fear that her presence is a result of a traumatic event in her life. This is quite common in Seekers, as they often suffer great loss before coming to the Truth. Many have died spiritually because they believe they've been overlooked or forgotten by the One. But it is the world, not the One, who has rejected them. The seeker in our woods has been deeply wounded by manipulation, abandonment, and abuse. She questions the existence of a

God who would allow such things to happen to one of His children. Her wounds are so deep that she cannot see He's always been with her, and she could have turned to Him at any time. But she has come to trust only herself, so she is blinded to the Truth."

"Will she ever find it?"

"When she forgives those who have caused her great pain, her healing will begin. Then she will receive the Life and discover her true self."

"Is there anything we can do to help her?"

"We can continue to pray. Aside from that, we are doing all that we can by giving her the space she needs in which to search. She knows she's safe here and that she won't be judged or reproached. We have great hope. But the rest is up to her."

"I wish the world would learn to trust Him." I gazed longingly into the woods.

Mum's eyes grew bright, and her face was aglow as she watched the revelation of His love transform me. "The seed of faith has been planted in your spirit, my darling. Nurture and protect it, and it will yield much fruit."

I smiled as I imagined the Word as a watering can that poured out wisdom and truth over me and washed away all my doubts and fears.

"That's the way to start each day," I decided. Then another revelation came to me, and I jumped down from the window seat.

"Good heavens," Mum said, "what's the matter?"

"I'm starving!" I declared. With wide eyes and a mischievous grin, I challenged her to a race. "First one to the kitchen gets extra cream for their cobbler."

"You're on!" she cried out as I ran toward the door.

She quickly overcame the slight edge I had on her, and she nearly passed me when we reached the landing. I squealed with delight when I felt her close behind me, and I held out my arms to block her. Then I jumped over the bottom step and took off like a rabbit. She was less than a few inches behind me when we reached the kitchen, where Grammy was waiting by the door.

"The winner by a nose!" she announced as she raised my arm in victory.

"Oh, my heavens," Mum said, catching her breath. "She's one fierce competitor!"

"You came so close to beating me!" I laughed and gave her a big hug. "I love you," I said instinctively. "And I love you more than the whole wide world," I said to Grammy, who looked at Mum and winked, then she leaned down to kiss my cheek.

CHAPTER 19

GONE FISHIN'

My stomach rumbled as my attention turned to the food being placed on the table. "There's an extra place setting," I said. "Is someone joining us for breakfast?"

The voices in the yard answered my question, and I ran to the back door to see Daddy and Micah standing by the great oak tree. Micah was telling one of his stories, which made Daddy double over in laughter. Belly laughs made my father cry, and he wiped a happy tear from his eye just as I stepped onto the porch, letting the screen door slam behind me.

"Sorry!" I yelled to no one as I sped toward my father's open arms.

"Mira darling! How are you on this lovely morning?"

"Filled with faith and hope, Daddy."

Micah threw his head back and laughed as I ran to greet him. He reached for me and lifted me high above his head. I spread my arms out as if I were flying.

"You are full of spunk, little miss! Tell us what you've been up to that's filled you to the brim this morning."

Daddy and Micah acted surprised as I recalled every detail of the bunny tale with great enthusiasm. But from the corner of my eye, I saw Daddy nod and wink at Micah, and I remembered what Mum had said about witnessing my gifts long before I realized them.

"Your gifts are bearing fruit, darling," Daddy said. "It won't be long before creatures, great and small, come to sit peacefully by your side."

"Really?" I looked at Micah for confirmation.

He put his hand on my shoulder and nodded as we walked toward the kitchen for breakfast. Micah took a big whiff of the bacon that was frying on the stove as Grammy took the peach cobbler from the oven. He walked up behind her and gave her a hug. She giggled and blushed as she handed him a large plate and began placing the cobbler on it. He took a few long whiffs of the pastry and sighed.

"Petra, you are indeed a treasure. And I am privileged to be on the receiving end of one of your greatest gifts."

"Oh Micah! The pleasure is truly mine. You are our most precious blessing this morning and every other."

Mum appeared from the basement carrying a tray filled with homemade jellies and jams, which she placed on the table next to a basket of warm bread. Daddy had barely finished blessing our food when Micah began to share stories that were beyond belief, but nonetheless, true. He told us a tale of a man who died and was brought back to life after three days. And of another who lived in the belly of a whale until it spat him out on dry ground. There were stories of many people who had been healed from lifelong illnesses; the blind could see, the deaf could hear, and the lame could walk. I found myself secretly wishing that I could perform miracles in people's lives, and I held my desires close to my heart.

Micah and I took over the chore of cleaning up, so Mum and Grammy could spend time planning the garden they'd been talking about.

"Have a wonderful time, ladies," Micah said. "The little one and I will take care of everything."

"That was indeed a delicious breakfast. And wonderful conversation, too." Daddy said as he picked up the Word and headed to the porch. "Thank you, one and all, for starting this beautiful day in sheer perfection."

Micah and I finished the dishes quickly, while making sure there were scraps left for the wildlife. I wrapped them up in a sheet of waxed paper that I folded carefully on the top and sides then wrote in black ink, "Please do not eat."

Micah took the pen and added, "Unless you're a deer!"

We both laughed, as we knew Mum and Grammy would laugh too.

"It is a glorious day. What do you say we take the boat out on the lake?"

I had no idea why I would be troubled by it, but the mere mention of the lake sent a chill down my spine. I felt the color leave my face, and I was suddenly nauseous. Micah knew right away that something was wrong.

"Ah!" He gave me a wink. "You've never been to the lake before, right?"

I nodded and shrugged my shoulders. It was true that I'd never been to the lake. In fact, I'd never been near it.

The lake was quite a distance from the house on the hill and well beyond the borders of U-R-Here. It wasn't that it wasn't allowed to go there...it just wasn't a place that I cared to go. But at that moment, I wished Daddy would have forbidden me, as it would have given me a very good reason to stay where I was.

"Well, we'll have to clear it with your family first," he said, "but I'm sure it will be okay, especially since the water was very calm on my way here this morning."

I gave him a halfhearted smile, which only seemed to encourage him.

"I'm an excellent captain, by the way. You're in very good hands!" He smiled and winked, and the queasiness in my stomach suddenly disappeared.

"The thing is," he said, "the lake is truly awesome and something you really shouldn't miss. It's much bigger than the stream and pond that you're used to. But that just means it holds a zillion more treasures. There are fish, of course. Lots of fish! Trout. Perch. Shiners. There are also salamanders, frogs, lizards, and at least six types of turtles that are all different sizes and colors. The painted turtle is a work of art! You just have to see it." Micah's eyes were as wide as a child's on Christmas morning, and his enthusiasm made me forget that I was ever worried about going to such an incredible place.

"And there are amazing plants in and around the water," he went on. "One of my favorites are the giant waterlilies because they're exquisitely formed and float together in a cluster, like a giant floral bed. But there are other floating water plants too, like the hyacinth, poppy, and water lettuce."

"Okay, okay, okay!" I laughed and halted him with an outstretched hand. "I'm convinced!"

"Great!" He slapped his knees with both hands. "Now we just need your family's approval, and we'll be on our way."

"I can't wait!" I ran upstairs to change.

"Bring a hat," Micah called out. "It's likely to be sunny on the lake. But it might be cool. Bring a windbreaker just in case."

"Okay!" I yelled down the stairs.

"Long pants and sneakers too. We might want to go for a hike on the other side. And wear a T-shirt under a long-sleeved shirt. Layering is the way to go."

He smiled when I returned to the kitchen wearing everything he suggested and looking very overdressed.

"Lose the hat," he said jokingly as he shut the lid of a child-sized picnic basket.

"Wow! I sure hope both of us don't get hungry today." I laughed. The basket looked as though it wouldn't hold more than half a sandwich at most.

"No worries," he said. "There'll be more than enough and some leftover."

I was doubtful, but since I was still very full from breakfast, I wasn't too concerned about food.

Daddy dozed on the porch with the open book in his lap, which nearly fell to the floor when we walked through the door. Micah lunged to grab it before Daddy knew what had happened. Placing it back on his lap, Micah asked if he'd like to join us on the lake.

"No, no," he said quickly. "You two go off and have fun. I'm quite content to sit on the porch and read." He folded his arms and rested his head on the back of the chair. "Anyway," he added, "I'm starting to think there might be a nap in my future."

Micah chuckled, and I kissed my sleepy dad on the cheek and said good-bye. As we walked away from the porch, I turned and waved, but the wave was not returned.

"He's already snoozing," I said, with a smile.

"Good for him," Micah added. "He deserves a rest."

I followed Micah to a clearing on the side of the house that was a perfect spot to plant a garden. I had forgotten where Mum and Grammy said they were going, but Micah knew exactly where to find them. The Two were fully engaged in the planning of their garden when we arrived unexpectedly.

"Oh, my heavens!" Grammy said. "You nearly scared the daylights out of me."

"I'm so sorry, Petra," Micah said sincerely and gave her a big hug. Grammy kissed him on the cheek.

"That's quite all right, dear. We just reached a little stumbling block regarding the cucumbers, and we're looking for common ground. Perhaps you can help."

"Oh yes! You've come at the perfect time," Mum said as she shared their dilemma with us. "There are many different types of cucumbers, as you well know. We both agree on Armenian and Japanese for slicing, but we haven't yet settled on one for pickling. Grammy likes Kirby."

"You can't go wrong with a Kirby cuke," Micah said.

Mum was quick to add her choice.

"But I'm fond of heirlooms."

"Yup! They make one delicious pickle," Micah agreed.

"So...what should it be, Micah? Kirby or heirloom?"

Mum and Grammy looked like two little girls as they smiled and batted their eyes for his attention. I was expecting them to wave their hands or jump up and down saying, "Pick me! Pick me!" Micah stroked his bearded chin with one hand.

"Hmmm," he said thoughtfully and then decided, "plant them both."

"What a wonderful idea!" Grammy said.

"Yes," Mum agreed. "Why hadn't we thought of that?"

Then they turned toward the patch of earth they'd designated for planting and happily carried on. Micah attempted to share our plans for the day with them, but they were too engrossed in creating to pay attention.

"Yes, yes, dears," Mum said as she waved good-bye a bit too prematurely. "Have a wonderful day."

"Do you think they were glad to be rid of us?" Micah asked, after we said our good-byes.

"Oh my, yes!" I laughed. "The only time Mum and Grammy aren't easily disturbed is when they're planning a project. It can get ugly."

Micah cracked up at my description of a side not often seen in the world's most gentle, loving women.

"The good news is...whatever they plant will be amazing."

"They are remarkable," Micah said. And I agreed.

We walked down the hill and followed the stream away from U-R-Here until we came to shallow water. We stepped over some large rocks to the other side and then climbed up an embankment that led to a wooded area and finally to a clearing.

It took a while to get there, but when we arrived, Micah said, "Well…we're here! What do you think?"

I looked from beneath the boughs of the tallest trees I'd ever seen, past a sandy area with large rocks jutting out of the still water. The surface of the lake was several shades of blue and green, and the ripples that crept up to the shore left tiny pebbles behind. It was quiet and peaceful, and the only sound was that of an occasional chirp or whoop that came from the branches high above.

"It's magnificent," I proclaimed. I stood spellbound by the earth's splendor. "I've never seen anything like it."

"We've only just begun, little one. Follow me!"

I followed Micah down a small hill to a long dock that floated no more than a foot above the water. One small rowboat was tied to the dock, and for a moment, the annoying little knot appeared again in my stomach.

"Is that your boat?" I asked sheepishly.

"Yes, it is," he said cheerfully. "Isn't she a beaut?"

We walked to the dock, and Micah held my hand as I stepped into the boat. The swaying startled me, but Micah said, "Don't worry! You'll get your sea legs in no time!"

I sat down as soon as both feet were in the boat, and before long, I had settled in comfortably. Micah put the small basket of food behind his seat and untied the boat, pushing it away from its berth and into the vast waters in front of us. Grabbing hold of the oars, he rowed steadily toward the middle of the lake while I looked over my shoulder to see where we were going.

"You can turn around," he said. "It's much better to see where you're going than to watch where you've been."

The lake wasn't very large, not more than one hundred acres all told. But it was the most water I'd ever seen, and it seemed so vast. Micah rowed without ceasing until we were in the center of the lake. He pulled up the oars, and the boat came to rest. Surrounded by the deep blue-green water and the beautiful sky above, I was enveloped in an extraordinary peace. I glanced over my shoulder and smiled at Micah.

"You look as though you're enjoying yourself, little one. Why don't you turn around, so I can see your lovely smile?"

I decided to stand up and step over the seat, as I had a new confidence in my seafaring abilities. I gave Micah the thumbs-up sign, assuring him I had it covered, but as I sat down…he stood up and started applauding! The sudden movement set the boat to rocking, and I grabbed onto the seat and laughed uncontrollably as I bounced up and down. Micah grinned as he sat down, and the twinkle in his eye told me he had something up his sleeve.

"Let's go fishing," he said.

"Fishing? But we didn't bring any poles."

"We don't need poles," he assured me. "We just need a good invitation."

I tilted my head and crinkled my nose. "A good invitation?" I chuckled. "What do you mean by that?"

"You know…an invitation. This will be a bit tricky because you haven't met the lake fish yet. But I believe it will only take a few words from your sweet voice to coax them into the boat."

"Into the boat? Did you say, 'Coax them into the boat'?"

Micah laughed and nodded his head. "It'll be great! Just lean over the side, so they can see your face. Then invite them to join us."

"Ha-ha!" I laughed nervously. I'd never done anything like this in my life, so I had no idea how to invite fish anywhere, let alone into a boat. I giggled as I pondered the proper way to extend such an invitation.

"Don't worry about what you say," Micah offered. "Just speak to them the way you spoke to the ivy and the flowers. Sweetly! And don't be afraid. There's no right or wrong way to do this. You just have to start."

I chuckled again. "Okay, here goes!" I took a deep breath and nearly forgot to let it out. The boat tilted as I shifted to one side and leaned over the water. "Here fishy, fishy, fishy, fishy!"

Micah reeled back and laughed so hard, his pants nearly split. "What kind of invitation is that?" he chided. "'Here fishy, fishy, fishy, fishy'? Come on, child! You can do better than that. Try again. Only this time…put a little heart into it."

I gave him a crooked smile and leaned toward the water once again. "Hello to you, my dearest fish! Hello to all your friends! We would be so very honored if you would join us on our boat." The water was still, with no sign of life beneath the surface. I tried again. "Hello to you, my dearest fish! Hello to all your friends! We would be so very honored if you would join us on our boat." Still nothing.

"I know what the problem is," Micah said, after the third invitation. "You're inviting them from the wrong side of the boat."

I thought for sure he was joking. The boat was less than four feet wide. If the fish couldn't hear me on one side, how could they hear me on the other?

"No, seriously!" he urged. "Try it!"

I kept my eyes on him to make sure he wasn't sniggering as I slid slowly across the seat to the other side of the boat. But he wore only a reassuring smile; so I leaned over the side and repeated my invitation to the fish.

"Hello to you, my dearest fish! Hello to all your friends! We would be so very honored if you would join us on our boat." I looked at Micah and was about to tell him that I didn't think they heard any better on this side when—

Whoosh!

Flop!

Flop! Flop! Flop!

Whoosh!

Fish jumped into the boat by the dozens until the bottom was covered with every kind of fish imaginable. I squealed with delight as Micah laughed so hard, he almost turned us over. He held his sides and slipped backward, his legs flailing in the air as more fish flew into the boat. A few fish followed him and landed on his belly. Micah spit and sputtered as they slapped his face with their tails.

"Micah, make them stop!" I cried when we were suddenly up to our knees in fish. "The boat is going to sink if they keep coming!"

"You do it!" He chuckled, as he brushed a few flopping fish from his lap.

"Me? Oh, dear heavens! I don't know how to uninvite fish!"

He held his sides as he laughed even harder.

"Argh!" I cried, in complete desperation. I cupped my hands around my mouth and shouted into the water, "Stop!"

Instantly, the fish stopped jumping into the boat. My mouth dropped in amazement.

"Good job!" he said as we sat among the flailing fish. "Looks like we have lunch."

I was mortified. "Lunch? I'm not going to eat them!"

Again, he laughed. "Well, if we aren't going to eat them, we'll have to send them back."

"Good idea," I said, waiting for instructions.

But Micah said nothing. The fish weren't moving around as much as before, and I knew we had to get them back in the water. Micah watched as I reached down, picked up a fish by the tail, and flung it into the lake. More laughs from the other end of the boat.

"Micah, you must help me! Please! This is serious. They have to get out of the boat now, or they'll die."

"You're right," he said sombrely. "But can I just say something about what you've done here today? It was amazing! Truly amazing! You accepted instruction and my suggestion to go to the other side of the boat even though you didn't think it would work. And look what happened. You showed great wisdom, my dear. And faith! We can't overlook that. It's enormously important."

I believe I would have received his comment more fully had we not been sitting knee-deep in distressed fish. I leaned over our catch of the day to get closer to him. I wanted to make sure he heard me.

"Micah," I said, with wide eyes and a pleading smile, "the fish!"

"Okay. Okay. No worries," he assured me. "I've got this."

He sat with his knees spread apart and looked down at the fish as if to number them. "Fish," he said, "go."

At his words the fish began to flop and wiggle wildly as if life had just been spoken into them. They sprung up from the bottom of the boat like popcorn, then suddenly one jumped back into the water. Another followed. Then three...twenty...a hundred...until every fish was gone. Micah looked around the boat. Satisfied that they were all safe in the water, he turned toward the lake and smiled as a nice-sized perch jumped high above the surface and wiggled its tail. Micah waved a cheerful good-bye and then picked up the oars.

"Well," he said, with a big grin, "that was fun."

My eyes were as wide as saucers; I was too stunned to speak. I twirled around in my seat and stared off into the distance. We were getting closer to shore when I looked over my shoulder and smiled at my bearded friend. "That was amazing," I said.

Micah let out a big laugh. "It sure was, little one!"

And he kept rowing.

CHAPTER 20

AND THEN THERE WERE FOUR

I t took twice as long to get back to the house as it should have with Micah retelling the fish story along the way. We'd walk a short distance when he'd remember something else, and then we'd stop while he acted it out. He was so funny, both my stomach and face hurt from laughing. When we reached the back porch, I groaned at the thought of walking up a few steps. Micah shook his head and bent down to offer a piggyback ride.

"Really?" I hoped he wasn't kidding around.

"Sure! Hop on! But don't forget to duck when we go through the door, or we'll both be on the floor."

I climbed on Micah's back and wrapped my legs around his waist and my arms around his neck. His long hair tickled my nose and nearly made me sneeze.

"Hang on." He rose to his feet. "Here we go!"

Grammy and Mum were busy in the kitchen, and the table was already set for a party of many more than four. Micah bent down for me to climb from his back.

"Thank you, kind sir," I said with a curtsey. "The ride was greatly appreciated."

"You're welcome, Your Highness." Micah stood as he swept an imaginary hat from his head and took a regal bow. "I am always at your service."

Mum laughed as she stopped her busyness and joined in the fun.

"Well, hello, my dear princess," she said. "And a hearty welcome to you, good and faithful servant! Will we have the pleasure of your company for dinner this evening? I'm quite certain we can accommodate you both."

"Yes, ma'am, and thank you very much. We would be honored to sup with you this night. Isn't that right, servant?"

"Yes, Your Highness. Honored!"

Mum kissed my forehead as I ran to greet Grammy, who thanked Micah for spending the day with me.

"The pleasure was all mine, I can assure you," he said. "And I believe we might have a tale or two to share with everyone at dinner tonight."

Micah winked at Mum as her eyes grew wide and her beautiful smile filled up her face. "Well, we'll all be interested to hear about your day. But now, my darling daughter, you must get cleaned up for dinner. I dare say, Micah, you could do with some cleaning up as well. You both smell a little…fishy."

Micah and I broke into peals of laughter as we went our separate ways to prepare for the evening ahead.

The warm bath nearly put me to sleep as the fullness of the day was upon me. But my body was not nearly as tired as my heart was happy. And the idea of sharing this most remarkable day with my family and friends was more than enough to charge my battery for the evening ahead.

"I wonder what everyone else's day was like?" I thought as I finished dressing. "If it was anything like mine, we might be telling stories all night long!"

"Woo-hoo!" I shouted as I ran down the stairs and into the kitchen.

Daddy walked in from the porch just as I skipped in from the hallway. Our smiles were ear to ear as Daddy opened his arms out wide for me to run into. He lifted me up and kissed my cheek. We looked at each other and said, "Woo-hoo!"

"Well, well, well!" He chuckled as he lowered me back to the floor. "You and Micah must have had quite a day."

"Oh, we did, Daddy. It was remarkable!" I walked over to where things were cooking to see if there was something I could do to help. "But I don't want to give anything away until Micah gets here. He tells stories much better than I do."

Mum handed me four dinner plates and napkins, which surprised me, as it seemed the table was already set.

"They go to the picnic table in the yard, dear," she said. "Daddy will bring the glasses and silverware."

I was puzzled. The table always had room for more, so why would four people eat in the yard? I put the dinner plates and napkins on the table as Daddy stepped up behind me.

"Who is this for, Daddy?"

He put the glasses and flatware down and sat on the bench. "This is what we call our 'just-in-case' table, dear. It's for those who will eat our food but not with us. They've been invited many times. But the invitation only enrages them, and they become very indignant. We set a table for them and leave the door open. But it's up to them to come in."

"Are they seekers?"

"No, dear. It would be a blessing if they were. No. I'm afraid this group might be too lost to seek. But they've never spoken to us, so I don't know what their stories are. We decided long ago that there are those who will only retreat further into themselves when they see an outstretched hand. It is best to let them be and keep the door open. Just in case."

"Do you know who they are? Do they have names?"

"Yes, I'm quite sure they have names. But we don't know them. There are two women and two men. I don't think they speak to one another, although they do speak at each other."

"What do you mean, 'at each other'?"

"Well...it's obvious that one of the gentlemen...the one who always stands at attention and never has a single hair out of place...detests one of the women. He doesn't like the others either, but his disapproval of this one is as subtle as an elephant on roller skates. He has been heard saying things like, 'It's a shame we don't all rule the world like the Grande Dame, here,' or, 'If I had a dime for every time she did the right thing, I still wouldn't have a dime.'"

I chuckled even though I knew he wasn't trying to be funny. "Does she say anything?" I asked, wondering if she ever defended herself.

"No. His presence is irrelevant to her, so she chooses not to notice him or anyone else, for that matter. She has placed herself high above them and believes they're insignificant. I'm afraid some people can only feel good about themselves when they make others feel worthless. I believe that somewhere in the world, she is very powerful and accustomed to having her way. She simply won't accept that this is not the way things work here. She sits in her place at the head of the table and rings a little bell to let everyone know she's waiting to be served. The food is on the table in front of her, but she won't lift a finger to help herself. None of the others will lower themselves to put food on her plate, so it usually remains empty."

"Usually?"

"Well…there have been occasions when the incessant bell ringing disturbs the houseguests. Micah or I have been known to excuse ourselves from the table and put something on her plate…before taking the bell away."

"You didn't!" I said in total surprise.

"Oh yes! We have, and we will. Not that we want to. But she leaves us no choice."

I laughed out loud at the thought of them snatching the bell from her. "What about the others?" I asked. "What are they like?"

"They're basically the same, as each one is driven by pride and fear. But the little round man has been spotted peeking through the window at the gathering having dinner. And Grammy thought she saw him lurking on the porch during grace one night. We live in hope and give thanks to the One for His grace and mercy. Unfortunately, the round one is controlled by the others, and he seems to need their approval for everything. So, he does whatever he thinks would please them even though it would take a miracle for them to acknowledge his efforts. They're far too self-absorbed to notice how hard he works for their attention. To them he is nothing more than a buffoon who exists for their bidding, and they consistently make him the brunt of their jokes. We all feel very sorry for him, but it's not our place to intercede. We continue to pray that he will find the courage to stand against the will of man and find peace that comes from accepting the One into his heart."

"Guard your heart with all diligence," I said, recalling Grammy's lesson.

"Amen," my father said, before continuing his assessment of the four. "The angry man is the most difficult to love. He has tested us in that commandment more times than we can count. Still, we try to remember that even he was once a child, and we wonder what could have happened to have instilled so much hatred in him. He is very distrustful, that much we know. And furiously prideful! He holds himself in high esteem. In his eyes no one is more important than he is, and he treats everyone as if they are dirt under his feet. I believe he is exceedingly envious of whatever the woman he hates has. Most likely it is money and power, for those are the things he would covet. She has what he desires, and he believes she doesn't deserve them. Although somehow, he thinks he does."

Daddy frowned and shook his head at the ground.

"Another thing I've noticed about the angry man is that he's always dressed in a highly starched white shirt with a blue necktie knotted tightly around his neck, even in the heat of summer. I've often thought that if he dressed more comfortably, perhaps he would be happier."

He paused for a moment and then stood. "We should go in, honey. The guests will be arriving soon."

"What about the other woman, Daddy? Can you tell me something about her?"

I was desperate to understand the four who repeatedly refused friendship and kindness for the sake of arrogance and pride. My heart broke at the thought that they might not ever be free of themselves. Could anyone save them?

"Okay, honey." He smiled as he took his seat on the bench once again. "The other woman is a mystery. She doesn't appear to be wealthy or powerful. In fact, I would bet that she's quite common. Not poor. Just average. Like most of us. But I think she's also very smart. And therein lies the problem. She is likely much smarter than any of the others, yet she has not achieved the status or respect she believes she deserves. She looks down her nose at all of society and wallows in the conviction that she is a highly intellectual and cultural being who is far superior to most of the world. Knowledge is a wonderful thing, but not when it's only purpose is self-gratification."

"This breaks my heart," I said earnestly. "What made them the way they are, Daddy?"

"Oh, I don't know, honey. It could have been any number of things. Fear. Rejection. Abandonment. Entitlement. There's no telling what kind of demons they have encountered in their lives."

"I think they all have too much," I said in judgment. "Too much pride. Too much intelligence. Too much money."

"There is nothing wrong with abundance," he said, and I immediately felt very small. He gestured for me to sit beside him and then took my hand in his.

"Everything He created was meant to provide more than we might ever need or desire," he explained. His voice was kind and reassuring. "Just look around you. He hasn't skimped on anything. How many different types of trees do we need? How much sky? Could we ever count the colors that we see in a single day or number the stars at night? No. He is abundant in all that He does, and His pleasure comes from the glory He receives when we give Him thanks and praise. After all, we cannot do what He has done. And we do not own what He has given us. If we spend our lives pursuing possessions instead of the Provider, we will end our lives with nothing."

I knew that what he said was true, but my heart remained desperate for those who would never hear the words he spoke.

"But the very good news is this," he said with unwavering conviction. "We are so deeply loved and so greatly desired by the One that He waits for us. Just as a good father waits for wayward children to come home. He watches as we make bad decisions and choose poorly...even if it's throughout our entire lives. He waits with a heart that is broken by rejection from those He loves so dearly. He never leaves us. He never forsakes us. And, at the moment when we see the Light...even if it's before our final breath...He forgives us and rejoices as He welcomes us home."

An image of the One as a good and faithful Father filled me with hope, and the knowledge that we are so loved by Him that He never abandons us...even when we have repeatedly rejected Him...penetrated every cell and fiber within me. And this truth was suddenly as much a part of me as the air in my lungs or the blood in my veins.

Daddy looked down at our hands that were clasped together and shook his head.

"It all comes down to the lies the Enemy tells us about ourselves. He tells us we can do anything we want to do and be whatever we want to be. That we don't need to answer to anyone. He tells us we are the masters of our own fate and are fully sufficient in and of ourselves. He is the Great Deceiver, and he came to steal, kill, and destroy. The four people who sit outside at this table have bought his lies hook, line, and sinker. And yet...we pray. And set the table...just in case."

"But what will happen to them if they'd rather die alone than accept the kindness of strangers?"

My father sighed and shook his head as he heard the question he'd likely asked himself a million times. "What indeed?" he asked softly.

I closed my eyes and bowed my head as I prayed with my whole heart for their salvation. A tear slid down my father's cheek as he squeezed my hand.

"Let's go in, darling. We've done all that we can out here."

The house was spilling over with the sounds of laughter and conversation. After we were seated, and daddy said grace, Micah entertained the multitude with fish tales that were difficult for some folks to swallow. But there was no doubt in the minds of the happiest family that ever lived, as they had witnessed miracles far beyond what anyone could imagine, all by their faith in the One Who Provides.

Dinner sailed by that night and before we knew it, the guests had departed, and the kitchen was cleared. Micah and I took one final walk to the yard with a plate full of scraps for our woodland friends. We placed the food under the giant oak, and Micah blessed those who would be fed. Then we walked slowly toward the house, too tired to take long strides. When we got to the porch, Micah asked if I wanted to sit outside for a while.

"I know you're exhausted," he said. "But the air is too lovely to pass up this evening. Just a few moments?"

I nodded. "It smells like honeysuckle." I sat on the porch steps.

We sat in silence for a while, listening to the sounds of the earth and breathing in the cool night air. I rested my head on my knees and hugged my legs as my eyes fell closed.

"This was the best day of my life, Micah."

"Yup," he said, gazing into the evening sky. "Mine too." He turned to me and smiled. "Until tomorrow!"

I nodded happily.

"Was the picnic table empty tonight?" I asked.

"No. They were here. But they didn't stay. Too much laughter makes them uncomfortable, I'm sorry to say."

"Hmmm. Why do they choose to come at all?"

"That's an interesting question, little one. There certainly is no shortage of laughter around here. Maybe they're hoping we'll become as miserable as they are."

The air was still and quiet.

"Why would they want that?" I asked.

Crickets had begun chirping in the thick grass, and I heard an owl in one of the juniper trees.

"So, they can be right." Micah said.

Micah and I gazed toward the hooting owl as the words he spoke settled in our minds. We looked at each other and shook our heads.

"Not gonna happen," we said together.

My eyes began to close again, and I was suddenly too tired to move. Micah stood and lifted me up in his arms. He carried me to my room and tucked me in.

"Thank you," I managed to say, "for carrying me."

"You're welcome, little one. Sleep in peace."

And, I did.

CHAPTER 21

FAREWELL, OLD FRIEND

The warm sun streamed through my window and announced a new day. I jumped out of bed in the rumpled clothes I'd worn the day before and turned up my nose at the stale smell that spewed from them. "Whew!" I declared after sniffing my shirt. It smelled as though we were very busy yesterday. I quickly ran to the bathroom to wash away my funkiness before going downstairs.

"You are bright and early today," Grammy said, after giving me a hug. "Mmm! And as fresh as a daisy!"

"You should have smelled me when I got out of bed!" I laughed as I grimaced and pinched my nose. "Pee-yew!"

Grammy laughed as she smooshed my cheeks and planted a sweet kiss on my puckered lips. "Well," she began with a smile, "I'm very glad you cleaned up before breakfast. Fresh daisies are a welcome addition to our table."

She handed me a stack of dishes, spoons, forks, and napkins for four. I was a little disappointed that Micah wouldn't be with us for breakfast. I loved everything about life in

U-R-Here, but Micah made it exciting and fun. Maybe he would stop by later. I placed the plates on the table.

"Mira," Grammy said, "let's take a walk in the garden after breakfast. I'd like you to help me pick out the perfect flowers for Mrs. Kettle. The poor dear has been a bit blue the past few days, and I thought a lovely bouquet might lift her spirits."

"Okay, Grammy. Can I come with you to see Mrs. Kettle? Perhaps two of us could cheer her up twice as fast."

"That's an excellent idea, dear. Mrs. Kettle loves it when you visit. But we'll have to keep our eye on the time. I believe Micah is planning to stop by later this afternoon."

A big smile overtook my face just when Mum and Daddy entered the room.

"Well, well, well!" Daddy said teasingly. "What's given you a smile that stretches ear-to-ear? Did you hear your Mum and me coming down the hall?"

I giggled as he twirled me around by my finger as if I were a music-box ballerina. Mum came up beside me and kissed my cheek as I spun by her, and the day was officially underway.

"Daddy and I are going to take some things to the church this morning for a family who has just moved into the old Pritchett house in Anywhere," Mum announced, when breakfast was nearly done. "They're in need of just about everything, so we've packed up the truck and we'll head out right after breakfast."

"What are you giving them, Mum?"

"Things that have been very good to our family but that we don't use as much as we once did. Your cradle, for one. Daddy made that before you were born, and it served you well. But now it's time for it to be useful elsewhere. I know the family will be very grateful, as they are expecting a baby soon. Grammy made a beautiful quilt for the bed, and she knitted several sweaters and hats. The little one will be warm when the winter comes."

"Do they have any other children?"

"Yes, they do. They have a little girl who is about to turn three," Mum answered.

"Can I contribute too?" I asked, not knowing what I would give.

Mum, Daddy, and Gram looked at one another and smiled.

"Why, of course you can!" Mum said. "But we'd like to leave shortly, so if you're finished eating, you may be excused to find your gift."

"Thanks, Mum!" I quickly cleared my dishes from the table and then ran to my bedroom.

As I surveyed the room, I decided the perfect gift wasn't in plain sight. It was hidden away, like a precious jewel. The old wooden trunk that sat at the foot of my bed suddenly looked like a treasure chest, and I was certain that the most amazing gift was waiting inside. The hinges squeaked as I opened the lid, and the warm scent of cedar filled the air. The chest was chock full of soft woolen blankets, crocheted hats, knitted booties, and pure white linen pillowcases that were embroidered by hand and lovingly stored away for an infant who was yet to be. I lifted the neatly folded piles and put them on the floor next to me. I still didn't know what I was looking for…but I knew I would know it when I saw it.

An exquisite christening gown with matching bonnet and booties were wrapped in tissue paper and placed in a special box with a cellophane window on top. The box was sealed to protect the layers of lace from being damaged, but I saw small details of the dress through the translucent paper. I still didn't know what I was looking for, but I knew for certain this wasn't it.

A tiny brown-and-gold quilt lay beneath the box that held the christening dress. It didn't quite fit in with the rest of the contents in the hope chest, as everything else was delicate, and the quilt had a sturdiness to it. I was curious as to what was under its lovely patchwork. But at the same time, I sensed that the quilt was very much attached to what lay beneath it, and somewhat reluctant to let me go farther.

"My dear quilt," I said tenderly, "I know that you adore the precious treasure that you guard, for I believe I once loved it too. Just as I love you! I am so very sorry that I have waited so long to visit you. I do hope you'll forgive me. And grant me permission to remove you from the chest so I might behold the gift you covet."

I reached into the box and slowly lifted the quilt, then pressed it softly against my cheek. A familiar fragrance drifted past my nose, but the powerful scent of cedar made it difficult to detect. I closed my eyes and took a big whiff, hoping to awaken my olfactory memory. In an instant an image appeared in my mind that filled me with great joy and flooded my eyes with tears. My heart skipped a beat when I peeked into the old trunk and saw him laying comfortably in the basket I'd once turned into a bed. He looked exactly as I remembered...with long, floppy ears, soft, curly fur, and sad brown eyes.

"Spirit!" I gasped. I reached for the plush puppy that was once my faithful companion. I rocked him in my arms like a baby as I gazed lovingly at him. "I found you!" I said, swaying gently back and forth. "I'm so sorry that I left you alone for so long. Please forgive me!" I petted him gently behind his ear as I leaned down and kissed his nose. "Holding you now seems like the most natural thing I could ever do." I gazed into his eyes. "And…I'm not sure that I can let you go now that I've found you." I pulled him closer to me as I pondered this thought deep in my heart. "But you see… there's a little girl who has moved to Anywhere, and she's going to need a friend. Not just any friend. But the very best friend anyone could ever have. The kind of friend you were to me."

I wiped a tear from my eye with his furry paw and put his face next to mine. I thought about what it would be like if I kept Spirit instead of giving him away. "One thing is certain," I said to my stuffed friend, "you are not going back in the cedar chest!" I shut the lid of the trunk. "And if you stay here, you can sleep on my bed all day long."

I stopped rocking and looked down at my sweet Spirit, knowing that I wouldn't take him with me everywhere I went, as I once did. Leaving him on my bed as I went here and there without him would be nearly as cruel as leaving him in the chest—maybe worse.

"You deserve more than that, Spirit. You deserve to be properly loved." I hugged him very hard. "I will never stop loving you. And I will never forget you. But this new little girl needs you. She will love you more than the whole wide world. She is your new wish come true. And even though she doesn't know it yet…you're her wish come true too."

I looked into the sad eyes of my dearest Spirit and kissed his dark-brown nose. Then I wrapped him in the brown-and-gold quilt and headed down the stairs to the kitchen.

Mum gasped when she saw me holding Spirit in my arms.

Grammy whispered, "Oh, dear heavens!"

Daddy asked me if I was sure about giving Spirit to a child I'd never met, and I told him that she would know me by his love and that one day, we would have something very special in common that we could talk about.

No one said a word for a long time. They just smiled at one another and shook their heads. I knew they were fighting back tears because I was, too. Soon it was time for me to hand Spirit over to Mum and to a new life with a new little girl.

"We are not fond of good-byes," Daddy said, when he saw my hesitation. "They are far too permanent. But if you're ready, give him a kiss and say farewell, for you know you will see him again."

I held Spirit close to my heart. "This is only farewell, my dearest friend. Be happy in your new forever home. Know that you will always be with me."

Then with one last kiss, he was gone.

CHAPTER 22

THE ENEMY IS FEAR

G rammy and I cleaned up the breakfast dishes and got ready for our walk to the garden. I grabbed a pair of heavy gloves in case we picked some roses, and Grammy put a pair of shears in a large, shallow basket. Then we headed down the path near the woods. We hadn't gone too far when I thought I heard something rustling in the bushes and sensed someone was watching us.

"Grammy," I began as I gazed into the woods, "have you ever seen the Seeker? Not just her shadow. I mean…have you ever seen *her*?"

"Oh yes, dear! Many times! Especially when she was young. She was quite desperate to find the Truth then, and we were all very hopeful. She was close to receiving it several times. But something would block her, and she'd retreat for days, sometimes months. Your dad, mum, and I took turns standing watch every evening at dusk. That's when she was most likely to venture out beyond the woods. We didn't say anything to her, but we prayed and read the Word aloud, hoping it would bless her. She was such a beautiful child but so afraid. And it seemed that she was very lonely. That made me wonder if she had a family or if perhaps, she'd lost them. I don't know. But as she grew older, she would be away for prolonged periods of time. Your mum hoped she'd found the way to the Truth but seeing her this time makes me think she's become accustomed to doing things on her own and doesn't trust anyone who might offer help. She's built up thick walls around her heart. If she doesn't find the Word soon, I'm afraid she'll be lost forever."

We walked in silence until we came to the garden, which seemed to stretch out for miles, with colors that were exceptionally vibrant and brilliantly displayed. Everything was in full bloom, and the fragrance that hung in the air was like scented gossamer floating in the early-morning mist. Butterflies flitted through a field of black-eyed Susan, and hummingbirds gathered nectar from the hollyhocks and bee balm. I stopped to watch one of the tiny birds as it hovered magically beside the thin, lance-shaped leaves. The speed at which the hummingbird's wings moved back and forth made them almost invisible, yet its body barely moved at all. I leaned over to get a closer look and motioned for Grammy to join me. She crept silently beside me.

"Look at him, Grammy!" I whispered. "He's a miracle!"

Grammy smiled as we watched him gather nectar from the bee balm and then dart off to find another full flower. The beauty and wonder of nature overwhelmed me, and my heart overflowed with gratitude.

"I am so blessed," I said to Grammy, who was quick to agree.

She took my hand as we scanned the field for the flowers that were meant to bring a smile to Mrs. Kettle's face.

"Let's start with some tulips," Grammy suggested as she headed toward the long-stemmed blooms.

But I had already become enchanted with the daylilies, so we set out in separate directions. I had only walked a few steps when I felt something move beneath my feet. I stopped to look down and in an instant, I was frozen in place, unable to move as the jaws of a venomous serpent opened wide, with his head stretched toward me. He was trapped under my feet, which felt like dead weight. I could neither lift nor move them. Terror swept through me as my head began to spin. I tried desperately to scream for help, but my words were stuck in my throat. I searched for Grammy, but she was nowhere in sight. My legs felt like jelly and I was nearly overcome with fear when I thought I heard her cry out, "JESUS!" In an instant, Micah appeared before me.

"Don't be afraid, little one. I am with you."

The snake hissed as venom dripped from his fangs. I wanted to run, but my feet wouldn't move.

"Micah! I don't know what to do!"

"Just stand firm. He won't hurt you. He knows I'm here."

My heart pounded violently inside of my chest as the landscape around me blurred, threatening my equilibrium.

"Focus, little one. Look at me. And do not turn your eyes to him."

"But, Micah...I'm afraid. He's so big, and his fangs are so long!"

"He's big *because* you are afraid. The weapon he uses against you is your fear. The Enemy isn't what's under your feet…it's what is in your mind. Don't give him any territory. He has no authority over you."

I thought the snake had stopped moving and glanced down to see. Taking my eyes off Micah for an instant was all the Evil One needed to gain control. He hissed as his forked tongue flitted into the air. I once again felt him writhing beneath my feet. The violent pounding in my chest grew louder as every muscle in my body weakened.

"Micah!" I called out.

"Do not look at him," he said calmly. "Keep your eyes on me. We have already overcome him."

I closed my eyes and took a deep breath…then a few deeper breaths. Micah was now a heartbeat away, and I felt my strength returning when he took my hands in his.

"Stand firm, little one," he said as he tightened his grip. "We've got this!"

And I believed him. With everything that was in me, I believed him.

"Do you remember when we went fishing?" he asked.

My body trembled, but I stood firm. "Yes, I remember," I nodded repeatedly.

"You must speak to the snake as you spoke to the fish when you wanted them to stop coming into the boat. Be firm. And when you tell him to go…tell him to go in my name. Do you understand?"

The snake hissed loudly, but I dug deep within my spirit and summoned courage to come forth. I nodded. "I understand." The snake struggled.

"He will not harm you, little one. Speak to him firmly and tell him to go in my name. Do it now!"

I swallowed hard and cleared my throat, all the while keeping my eyes on Micah.

"Snake!" I demanded. "Go!" I was forceful and bold, but the serpent writhed even more, and I nearly lost my foothold.

"In my name!" Micah said firmly. "Tell him to go *in my name.*"

I nodded as I bit my lower lip. "Snake! Go! In His name!"

I instantly felt the snake move, but his strength was depleted. His power was shrinking, as was he. I looked down at my feet, and he was becoming smaller and smaller...until he was the size of an earthworm. There was nothing that was remotely frightening about him. His fangs were gone, and so was his venom. He was nothing. I couldn't believe that just a moment ago I was terrified of this insignificant little worm that now wriggled from under my foot and disappeared in the dirt. I looked at Micah and nearly collapsed as the terror that had overwhelmed me was now uncontrollable laughter. Unable to stand I dropped to the ground and sat cross-legged on the very spot where the serpent had been. Micah sat in front of me, his knees touching mine.

"What just happened?" I asked him.

"You just met the Enemy, little one. And what you saw when you defeated him is all that he ever was. But he's very clever. He uses people's weaknesses to his advantage. He is the Great Deceiver who wants nothing more than to steal, kill, and destroy. The only way to beat him is never to give him power. That weapon is within everyone's grasp, for it exists in our minds. Remember him as the meaningless worm that he is, for he will undoubtedly return. But the next time, he will have no control over you."

I lowered my head to my lap and gave thanks to the One for sending Micah to save me. I knew he would be with me forever. My heart was full of joy, gratitude, courage, and strength. I looked at my friend and smiled.

"We just beat the devil," I said.

"That we did, little one! That we did."

CHAPTER 23

THE WAY

Grammy stood on the porch waiting for Micah and me to return. She was overjoyed to see us, and we were overjoyed to see her too. We hugged each other tightly and praised the One altogether. She said she never doubted the outcome of my encounter with the Enemy, as she knew the Spirit was with me and that I'd been given the heart of a warrior. Still, the waiting was long, and she was glad it was over.

"We must all face evil in our lives," she said. "And when we do, we must choose either to give in to temptation or stand against it. It is in a moment of indecision that the Enemy gains territory that he has no right to, by claiming we have freely given it to him. Your strength and courage will grow every time you say no to the lies he tells you and yes to the truth in the Word. For you know that His plans are to prosper you and never harm you. And He's faithful to His promises, as they are all yes and amen."

Micah smiled at Grammy and gave her a big hug. "You are such a blessing, Petra! I thank the Father every day for putting this child in your faithful hands."

Grammy's eyes were as bright as the stars on a cloudless night as she wiped away tears of joy from her face. "I am honored," she whispered.

Micah stayed for lunch, and we waited for Mum and Dad to come home to tell them of our brush with the Enemy. They had questions only Micah could answer, and I almost felt left out of the conversation, but Daddy kept me close beside him and assured me that everything would make sense soon.

"I know this is confusing, sweetheart. But the pieces will all fit together and when they do, you'll look back on your time in this place and realize this was your "Aha!" moment. When that happens, nothing will stop you from being who you were created to be, and you will do all that you were created to do."

I went to bed early that night, exhausted from the events of the day. After Mum tucked me in, Daddy and Gram came in my room to say good-night. Everyone's eyes were moist with tears that didn't spill over but remained puddled near the edges of their lower lids. It was as though they wanted to keep the emotions they felt inside them, unwilling to let them go too soon. I fell asleep as soon as my bedroom door closed and slept soundly through the night.

The house was unusually quiet when I awoke, and I nearly skipped the ritual of washing my face and brushing my teeth to see where everyone was. I puffed into my cupped hand to check my breath and quickly decided to stick with the routine. Standing in front of the bathroom sink, I checked again for a way to open the medicine cabinet. But my curiosity had turned into a habit, and I decided not to give it a second thought. Whatever was behind that door wasn't worth breaking a rule for. I knew that I would never think about it again.

I hurried out of the bathroom, changed my clothes, and went downstairs. I expected the smell of breakfast cooking on the stove to meet me on the way, but there was nothing in the air, and no one in the kitchen.

Where could everyone be? Then I saw the note in Mum's handwriting taped to the fridge.

Dearest One,
You needed rest, so we let you sleep in and have gone to the market. Micah stopped by with a picnic lunch and said he would wait for you in the meadow. This is a very special day. Take in every moment. We shall miss you, darling!
All our love,
Mum, Daddy, and Grammy

I smiled at the phrase "take in every moment" as I folded the note and stuck it in my pants pocket. They didn't miss a single opportunity to do that! I shook my head and glanced at the clock. Holy cow! It was 1:46 p.m.! Ha! No wonder I was starving! I ran through the kitchen door and to the meadow, hoping Micah was still there.

"Hey, sleepyhead!" he called out when he saw me. "Glad you could make it!"

I was overjoyed to see him. "Oh, Micah! I'm so sorry. Have you been waiting long? You must be starving. I can't believe you brought a picnic lunch. That was so very kind. I'm so happy you're here!"

Micah laughed at my overzealous entrance and motioned for me to join him. I smiled and plopped down on the blanket that was spread out under a giant sycamore. He opened the lid of the tiny basket he'd brought on our fishing trip. My jaw dropped, and my eyes opened wide as a veritable feast appeared from inside the miniature basket. All my favorite fresh fruits and vegetables from the garden, plus fried chicken, homemade chocolate cake, and a big container of ice-cold lemonade were spread out before me. I gasped.

"What's the matter?" Micah asked. "Did I forget something?"

"Plates," I said jokingly.

"Oh, that's right." He reached into the basket once again and pulled out plates, forks, knives, cups, and two red-and-white-checkered napkins.

"That should do it," he said.

I shook my head in amazement. There simply was no one like him. What had I done before knowing him? But thinking back, I couldn't recall a single moment when he wasn't there. It was as if I'd known him all my life, and I didn't want it to be any other way. We chatted as we ate, and Micah shared more stories of his journeys with a group of friends he referred to as "the boys." They all seemed like very ordinary people who did extraordinary things when Micah was with them. I certainly could relate to that. I told Micah I would very much like to meet them one day. He said they had said the same thing about me. Knowing that Micah had told his friends about me was impossible to get my hands around. To think that the most remarkable person who ever lived remembered me every day was immeasurably humbling. My heart was just too small to hold it all in.

"I have something very special planned for today," Micah said, through a mouth filled with pickles. "I thought we'd take a walk in the woods. It might be the only place we haven't covered in our adventures."

"The woods?" I was surprised that he had chosen the woods. Unlike the lake I was strictly forbidden to go near them. Daddy said the woods were not safe for little girls, and until now, I had no interest in venturing near them. But today was different. Today, I was with Micah. And he made me fearless.

"Did you ask Daddy if it was okay?" I hoped he did and that it was.

"I did." Micah took a bite of chicken. "And it is."

"Yay! I can't believe I'm going to the woods! I've always wondered what was there." I was too excited to take another bite.

"There's an amazing path that winds through the trees, passes over the stream, and leads to the most spectacular sight you will ever see. You can't even imagine how remarkable it is, and I can't begin to describe it. You simply have to believe it to see it."

"See it to believe it," I said, to correct him. He smiled and gave me a wink; and I knew I was in for an amazing adventure!

"What about animals?" I asked. "I know the deer live there, but what others are there? Do you think we'll meet them?"

"It's quite possible," Micah said. "But whether we meet them or not, you can be sure they'll be watching us."

I grew more excited about our journey and began to fidget. Micah laughed at my enthusiasm. After finishing his last bite of lunch, he packed the leftovers in the basket as I folded the blanket.

"Let's leave everything here," he suggested. "We'll pick it up on the way back."

Micah's path that would take us through the woods was quite a distance from where we had lunch, and it took a while to get there. The trees and underbrush we passed on the way to the clearing were inconceivably thick and dense. "It would take a miracle to get through that forest," I thought as we meandered farther away from the house on the hill. But Micah promised that our trek would be well worth the effort; so, I traveled happily beside him until he stopped in front of a spot that was no less dense than the woods we'd passed.

"Here we are!" he said cheerfully.

"Here we are?" I queried, searching high and low for an opening. "Where is *here*?"

"The path is here. So, that's where we are. We are here at the path."

"Micah, I don't see a path. All I see are trees and bushes and vines!"

"Tsk, tsk, tsk. Where is your faith? Do I have to take you back to the boat for another fishing lesson? Trust me, little one. The path is right in front of you."

I looked around again and sighed. "But...*you're* right in front of me," I said exasperated.

"Exactly." He grinned. "I am the Way! Follow me!"

His words were no sooner spoken when the trees parted before him, and Micah walked into the forest, with me on his heels. The trail was set by every step he took, as no one had ever set foot on this ground before. Vines and bushes separated to reveal a passage by which we traversed, for no obstacle dared stand in our way. The trees and vines formed a canopy over our heads, and streams of sunlight passed through the branches and leaves.

"We're almost there," he said. "Just a few more steps."

One. Two. Three.

The trees opened wide, and we stood side by side gazing out at a massive canyon that laid before us. It stretched through and down the mountain in colors that were indescribable, and my eyes could not hold the glory they beheld. The sun burst brilliantly over the richness of the earth to reveal the internal splendor she held within. My breath left me as I fell to my knees in awe of her beauty, and I bowed to the One Who Is, Was, and Always Will Be. The Creator of all things.

Micah looked out over the canyon and smiled. "He did this all for you, you know. He did this for all humankind."

I knelt at his feet, my face to the ground. Tears flooded my eyes and poured over the crimson canyon rock beneath me. Micah bent down and took my face in his hands.

"Why do you cry, little one?"

"Because I am not worthy," I stammered, unable to look at him.

"But you are. You are worthy because you are His. He knew you long before He formed you in your mother's womb. He created you for a purpose. You are part of His plan. You are beautifully and wonderfully made by Him and for Him. No one else can be you. And you can be no one else. The time has come for you to know how the Father sees you, so you can live your life as He intended, without fear of the world or a desire to be of it. You are a daughter of the Most High God. He has blessed you with many gifts that will serve His kingdom. Trust me. And have faith. The Father knows your heart, dear. He wants you to know it, too."

I fell into his arms in full surrender as a world of sadness that I'd hidden deep within my heart was lifted. Micah held me for a long time, rocking me gently back and forth, until I was able to stand on my own. Then he looked down at my tear-stained face and asked, "Are you ready?"

"Yes," I nodded.

"Good," he replied, lifting me to my feet. "I want to give you something before we leave here." Micah gathered some dirt in the palm of his hand and spit into it, making a rich mud. "Close your eyes," he said. He placed the wet earth on my eyelids with the tips of his fingers. Then he prayed. "Father, give Your daughter eyes that see all the wonder You have placed in her, so she may walk boldly into the Kingdom in Your name. Amen."

A stream of tears ran down my face, and with it all my pain and brokenness. The old was washed away, and I was made brand new. Born again. And this time, the Father was with me when I arrived. I lifted my face to the Light.

"Your name isn't really Micah, is it?"

His tender eyes sparkled as he took my hands and held them to his heart.

"No, dear," he smiled lovingly. "But then...your name isn't Mira either."

Nothing could have prepared me for this moment of complete and total awareness of who I was and how much I was loved by the Father and the Son. My body trembled from joy that could not be contained. I took a deep breath and filled my lungs with air so pure that it made me dizzy. My heart sent a rush of life-giving blood coursing through my veins. I was transfixed by His glory, spellbound by the Light that burned within Him. And when I gazed into His eyes…I saw myself for the first time.

CHAPTER 24

THE TRUTH

I can't claim to know how we came out of the woods that day. One moment we were standing before the great canyon, and the next we were in the meadow. It was Him, of course. The man I knew as Micah. It was always Him.

As we walked along the woods, I heard a rustling and thought it might be the Seeker. I grabbed Him by the arm, and we both froze.

"Listen," I whispered, my finger to my lips. "Did you hear that?" But there was nothing.

"Did you think it was the Seeker?" He asked.

I nodded. "Yes."

"She's gone," He said softly.

Mum's words about the Seeker leaving when she stopped believing came back, and my heart was heavy.

"When did she leave? Why did she go?"

"The other night, when you set the picnic table for those who wouldn't come in, she watched you from behind the trees. She was troubled because you were being kind to them. You see…she knew the four and she's held each one in contempt for a very long time. But the angry man and the woman he detests had both wounded her deeply, and she couldn't forgive them for the pain she endured at their hands. She chose, instead, to carry the scars of her woundedness as reminders that she is unworthy of love, and must not expect too much from the world, lest she'll be disappointed."

I felt as if I'd just been torn in two, and I searched Micah's face for answers. He took my hand and stroked it gently as we walked slowly through the meadow.

"When she was a child," he explained, "the Seeker tried to befriend the angry man. They were only ten years old at the time. She was a sweet, tender-hearted little girl who was sensitive to people's feelings, and she knew he was bullied every day by some very cruel boys. He was lonely and afraid, and he desperately needed a friend. But the Enemy deceived him into believing that the Seeker wanted to make a fool of him; so instead of accepting her gesture of kindness, he turned against her. He continued to be bullied throughout his life and he placed the blame for every blow he withstood squarely on the Seeker. You see…the angry man is a coward who doesn't have the capacity to examine his own behavior and be accountable for it. His pride will not allow him to admit when he's wrong. His obsession with the Seeker grew, until one day, a door of opportunity was opened, and he had to choose between compassion and revenge."

Micah paused and kissed my hand. I could barely breathe as I waited for the story to continue. My eyes cried out in desperation as anguish filled my heart.

"What did he do?" I asked.

"Pride is a monstrous sin, little one. It binds people to themselves and blinds them from the Truth. There is no hope for those who hold onto pride and reject the Light. I'm sorry to say that the angry man is filled with it."

I was overcome with sorrow for the man who was without a single friend and whose vengeful heart might never be mended. But I ached for the plight of the Seeker, and I needed to know what happened to her. Micah answered my questions before I could ask them.

"As is true of all cowardice, the angry man could not confront the Seeker face-to-face. He chose, instead, to hurt someone she loved. He did a lot of damage, and she cannot forget his hateful acts. But she has the capacity to forgive in her heart, and when she finds it, it will empower her. Never give up hope, little one. And know that the Father is always for us...never against us."

I hung on his every word with great expectation, as I suddenly understood the power of faith and prayer. A flood of gratitude washed over me for the unrelenting love that covered the Seeker over the years, and for the family that prayed for her every day without judgment or reproach. My heart was overflowing, but my mind reeled with questions I had yet to broach. They were difficult questions. And I was afraid that the answers might be too painful to hear. I looked at Micah who waited...so tenderly and patiently... until I found the courage to speak.

"The hated woman," I began. He squeezed my hand. "What did she do to the Seeker?"

Micah gathered me in his arms and pressed my head to his chest. I could hear his heart beat as he stroked my hair and held me tightly. There was sadness in his voice as he spoke.

"Evil exists in the world, little one, and in people. I'm afraid the woman is one of them. She has manipulated others for self-gain and in the process, she has destroyed many lives. But no one has been more severely wounded by her cruelty than the Seeker. The woman took the Seeker in when she was an orphaned child with nowhere to go and no one to care for her. Her deeds were considered honorable, at the time, and she was lauded for her compassion and charity. But her motives were far from altruistic, and the child soon fell victim to the woman's evil schemes and desires. The Seeker became her prisoner as well as her slave. She wasn't permitted off the property, nor was she allowed to interact with anyone who ventured near. The woman derived great pleasure from taking everything she could from the Seeker and robbing her of her dreams and desires. The Seeker had no hope for anything more from life and believed she'd been forgotten by the world. The woman had convinced her that she would never be able to survive without her; and the child lived in constant fear."

"Why didn't anyone help her? People must have known something was wrong!"

"There were some who questioned the situation, but the woman denied allegations against her. And, since there was no proof of wrongdoing, there was nothing that anyone could hold against her. And, of course, she was an exceedingly wealthy and very powerful person whose influence could make or break most people. No one was willing to take the risk; even if it was for a helpless child."

Micah held onto my hand as he sat down on the cool grass and led me to his lap. My head rested against his chest as he cradled me in his arms. The most difficult question lingered on my lips, but I was unable to speak what my heart needed to know.

Where was the Father in all this? How could He allow His beloved child to endure such pain and suffering? Why didn't He rescue the Seeker from this cruel fate?

Micah held me close as I struggled with questions that seemed to have no acceptable answer. His own heart had been broken many times by those who would not believe in something they could not see and refused a love they could not touch.

"We must learn to trust Him, little one. This can be difficult in times of trouble, and when the world seems to be falling down around us. But, in the most harrowing times, we must remember that He has a plan for each and every one of us. And His plan is not to harm us...but to proper us; to give us hope and a future."

I curled up closer to him as he gently rocked me in his arms.

"The Seeker's parents knew and loved the Father and the Son with their whole hearts. Their passing was premature and they were deeply grieved. In their final prayers, they asked the Father to provide abundantly for the child they would leave behind, and that He would lead her to her life's purpose. Many things that happened in the Seeker's life are unconscionable in the eyes of man; but they have prepared her for what is yet to come. The Seeker's gift of imagining worlds and circumstances that were far beyond her own experiences is what led her to this place and to this family. And…with the help of her only child…it will lead her to her life's purpose and the destiny that awaits her in His Kingdom."

In an instant, I was aware of all that was around and about me…and the knowledge of who I was and why I was born saturated my body, soul and spirit. I searched Micah's eyes for affirmation of what I already knew to be Truth, and I was suddenly drenched with a love that would bless all humankind. My gifts were meant to further His Kingdom… and my mother was meant to be with me.

"Mommy!" I gasped, as Micah stood and swept me up in his arms. His strength kept me from succumbing to an overpowering sense of urgency that threatened to overwhelm me, and I knew He was going to lead me home.

"Are you ready, Lily?" He asked with a grin.

"Oh, yes! Yes! I'm ready! But how? How do I get there from here?"

"The same way you came in, little one. Down the hill… by the stream…and through the meadow."

My arms were wrapped around his neck and I held onto him with everything that was in me. I never wanted to let him go.

"I'm not going anywhere," he assured me. "I'll never leave you nor forsake you. Whatever you need, ask in My name, and it will be given. If you need courage…ask for courage. If you need strength…ask for strength. My Spirit dwells within you, Lily. And there is nothing that can take my Spirit from you. I am always within…and you're never without."

I smiled, knowing he would always be the voice that would speak somewhere near my heart.

"Thank you, Micah!"

"My pleasure, little one. Now…are you ready to go?"

"Oh, yes! But…what about Mum and Gram and Daddy? Won't they wonder where I went? I mean…I should at least say good-bye."

Micah turned toward the only house on the only hill in U-R-Here, where Daddy, Mum, Grammy, and little Mira stood waving from the porch.

"Wave to them, Lily. They aren't fond of good-byes."

"I love you," I called out as I blew a kiss through the air.

"We love you!" they all replied.

And sweet Mira added, "As much as the whole wide world!"

I gasped when I heard her beautiful voice, and I waved one final farewell.

"I'm ready," I said.

And just as quickly as I found myself in U-R-Here…I was gone.

CHAPTER 25

THE LIFE

I opened my eyes slowly and squinted at the bright white light above my head. A pungent aroma passed beneath my nose and made me flinch. "Phew! Bleach!"

The sunlight poured through the sheer curtains, adding to the difficulty I had in adjusting my sight. I shut my eyes and turned away from the window. When I opened them... she was there...sleeping in a brown Naugahyde chair next to my bed. Her arms were wrapped around a book that lay on her chest as if it were a lifesaving device. She looked out of place curled up in a chair that wasn't her own. But far more than that, she looked tired. And, oh, so tiny and frail. The waiting had taken a great toll on her, yet she stayed by my side.

"I'm so sorry, Mommy," I whispered.

The sound of my voice was like a signal sent straight to her heart, and she awoke instantly. The book dropped to the floor as she unravelled herself from her awkward position and squinted at the bright morning light.

"Lily?" she asked as she shielded her eyes with one hand and reached for me with the other.

The sound of her voice paralyzed me, and I was unable to move or speak.

"Lily?" she asked again as she clutched my hand.

My eyes were flooded with tears as I nodded my head and smiled. She threw her arms around me and buried her face in my chest.

I wanted her to know this moment was real. I swallowed as hard as I could and cried out, "*Mommy!*"

"Oh, my dear Lord! Thank you! Thank you! Thank you!" She smothered me with kisses as her hands touched my face. "Oh, Lily! My Lily! He sent you back to me. Thank You, God! Thank You, Jesus!"

We held each other for a long time as she traced the fingers of my hands and breathed in the fragrance of my hair. I soaked in her voice, her sobs, her breath, her touch, her tears. We were drenched with the love that we knew was a gift and overwhelmed by the undeniable truth that only God could have done this. When hope had departed, and faith was nowhere to be found, He was there. His love saved us both.

My mother sat on the edge of the bed, staring at the book that had fallen to the floor. She picked it up and opened it to a place that had been marked with tears. She shook her head in disbelief.

"I had reached a point where I nearly gave up." She looked down at the book, and her right hand swept lovingly across the page. "The doctors didn't know what was wrong with you, so they couldn't treat you. I begged them to help you, but there wasn't anything they could do. They said there was no medical reason for why you wouldn't wake up. I didn't know what else to do, so I got down on my knees and I prayed. For hours, I prayed. I didn't eat or sleep. The hours turned into days, and I was so angry at God; I demanded that He tell me why my little girl was lying unconscious in a hospital bed and why He never answered my prayers. He didn't answer them when my parents died. He didn't answer them when your father left. And He wasn't answering them now. I fell asleep that night from sheer exhaustion and unbearable pain. I had a dream. In my dream I saw Jesus carrying you when you were too weak to walk. I didn't know what it meant. The next day one of the nurses gave me a Bible and told me a story of a man named Jairus whose daughter had died, and Jesus brought her back to life."

She took a marker from the book and handed it to me. "She gave me this as well."

I looked at the paper that had been folded and unfolded many times. I smiled as I pictured my mother pondering the words that were written in faded blue ink.

"Read it," she said softly. "It's from the book of Mark."

I closed my eyes and pictured the Seeker darting back and forth in the woods of U-R-Here, searching desperately for the Truth that I now held in my hand. "Praise you, Father," I whispered before reading the passage aloud:

Therefore I tell you, whatever you ask for in prayer, believe that you have received it, and it will be yours. (Mark 11:24)

"When I read those words," she said, tears streaming down her face, "I knew that Jesus would save you and bring you back to me. I had no doubt. And here you are."

My eyes hadn't stopped crying since I first opened them to the light. We laughed at what a mess we were. I handed her a tissue to wipe her eyes, but, instead, she wiped mine.

"*Lily!*" she cried as she clutched her heart. "What happened to your eyes?"

"My eyes? I don't know. What's wrong with my eyes?"

"Oh my heavens!" she exclaimed. "They're emerald green!"

I instantly felt Micah's fingertips covering my eyes, and I heard him say, "I want to give you something before we leave here."

I looked toward the heavens, although I knew that He was there with me. "Thank you. Thank you for this gift! Thank you for your love! Thank you for your Spirit! I will never, ever forget... You are always within. And I am never without."

My mother sat in awe as she gazed into the face of the miracle before her.

"Mommy"—a wise grin took hold of my face—"I think you should get comfortable. I have a story to tell you."

Her beautiful smile warmed my heart as she curled up next to me in bed, and I began the tale that she would never end.

"Did you know," I asked as my emerald eyes twinkled brightly, "that there once was a girl who had no reflection?"

EPILOGUE

J ules and Lily Johnson packed their belongings and left Lindenwood the day Lily was released from the hospital. Lily's heart broke when she learned that Spirit would not be coming with them. The days that Jules spent away from the cottage left him without anyone to care for him; so Jules made the very difficult decision to find him a good home. And that, she did. Spirit went back to the farm where he was born and was surrounded with love. Lily was filled with gladness as she imagined him with his new wish come true, and she carried him in her heart forever.

The two didn't know where they would go or what they would do. But their trust was in the One who brought them back together, and their journey was in the hands of the One with the plan.

The last rays of sunlight broke through the branches of the giant elms as they drove down the path toward the front gate.

"Make a note of the time that we pass through the entrance," Jules said as she kept her eyes on the road ahead.

"7:14 p.m.," Lily noted, when the tail lights had cleared the gate.

"7:14 p.m." Jules reached for her daughter's hand. "Life has just begun," she said with a smile.

"Amen," replied Lily.

And the two never looked back.

But small is the gate and narrow the road that leads to life, and only a few find it.

Matthew 7:14 (NIV)

ABOUT THE AUTHOR

A native of New Jersey, Linda Lee Bowen was raised in the Christian & Missionary Alliance Church and gave her life to Christ at age seven. She loved Sunday school and her teacher; but, mostly…she loved Jesus. She got caught up in the world at an early age and traveled throughout the country as a professional singer for several years. Tired from the road, she settled down in her hometown in her late twenties, got married, and began a career that lasted nearly twenty years in concept development and marketing. In those years, she had two sons who gave her life meaning and brought her immeasurable joy. But something was missing; she felt incomplete. That something was her faith. At age sixty, she was baptized in water and in the Holy Spirit. Five years later, she wrote *A Face Without a Reflection,* which she hopes will be a blessing to anyone who struggles with why they were born, and thinks they aren't lovable enough for God. Nothing could be farther from the truth. He knows our hearts because He created them. And He sees the beauty that lies within each and every one of us.

www.ingramcontent.com/pod-product-compliance
Lightning Source LLC
Chambersburg PA
CBHW070550130626
46556CB00001B/104